Disappearing Women

Disappearing Women

Cover illustration: Original artwork by Barbara Knight

Proofing and typesetting: Ryan Curtis and Julia Knight

Published by: Sculptural Images

Printed by: Ingram Spark

Dedication

This book is dedicated to my strong granddaughters

Zara Pritchard

and

Phoenix Bewsher

I know they are coming but don't know how long I must wait; how much longer I shall be allowed to live.

There is a soft mist filling the valley and I can see the city lights below glowing softly as through a flimsy curtain.

I pull my ugly brown burlap cloak around me, but I'm still shivering. I tell myself it's because of the cold but really I know it is fear the chills my bones and causes my old yellow teeth to chatter.

Is there anything I can do to escape what I know is coming?

Should I pack some food and clothes and head up the mountain, hide in the cave Amy and I found many years ago and live like an aged, feral creature? Would they hunt me down with dogs and guns or would they just wait until I crawled out starving from my time in the bush then dispose of me as they would any strange wild animal.

These questions reel through my head, but realistically I know I haven't the will or the energy to do anything but wait. I was the same all those years ago when I had my chance to escape. Fear and age stopped me then as it does now. I will fight them though when they come for me. I will not go meekly into their big car to be taken away to that ugly grey building, a place of death. I'm not going there. I'll kick and scream even though I know anyone who might hear me would be too fearful to intervene.

I don't know if I had some premonition of what was going to happen to me or it is simply coincidental but a week ago I began writing a journal detailing all that has happened to me during my long life and the changes I have witnessed in our society. All I need do now is add this last little bit then put the completed manuscript on a USB stick before clearing everything from my computer. When they come they mustn't see what I have written.

My hope is that this document will be read some time in the future and act as an explanation of the way in which our society changed to those who come after.

I cannot leave it for Jill. Ali would be sure to insist on reading it first and would destroy it. He would not want Jill to know what he has condoned. I will wrap it in a parcel addressed to Amani. Perhaps she will be able keep it safe.

2070

This was how I spent my day when I started this journal. I had been to the Centre until late afternoon and when I left there I walked the two blocks to the plant nursery, for I wanted to buy some broccoli and pak choi plants. The rain that had threatened earlier in the day held off and I felt quite warm in my thick burlap cloak as I made my way along the footpath.

The streets in town are so quiet now compared with how they were when I was a young woman. In part this is due to the changed traffic. Vehicles powered by electricity have replaced noisy petrol cars and diesel buses, and they are silent except for the swish of tyres on the road.

The other reason why the streets are now so quiet is because very few women are to be seen walking along the pavements. Those who had ventured outside their homes today passed by silently, singly or in groups like dark shadows. I smiled to myself thinking of how, in the past, we were the noisy ones, laughing and gossiping together, or chatting encouragement to children tired from the hurly-burly of a day in town.

Now the only women you see laughing in the streets are the Madams in their rich purple gowns and shawls. Often three or four of these women walk together when they go to the Correctional Centre to make their selections from the new arrivals. They don't fear the Militia officers the way the rest of us do. They know most of them, and their individual peculiarities and perversions.

They are the exception though, the only women who are at ease on the city streets. Most of us feel we are trespassing in the domain of men.

I passed a café where my girlfriends and I used to meet for coffee. It is still there and reminds me of the innumerable coffee houses Bill and I saw during our trip through Italy. Those places were also full of men, and Bill and I noted the absence of women.

On our travels we saw women working in the vineyards, fields and orchards, herding a gaggle of geese across a road or hanging out enormous amounts of washing on balconies or makeshift clotheslines. They seemed to be working so hard compared with the men who we saw idling their days away in those delicious smelling coffee houses. Bill and I joked that in Italy the women worked and the men drank coffee.

Now in our country the men work, but they also fill the coffee houses and restaurants while the women remain hidden away, their lives limited to caring for their children and homes.

As I passed the café I sniffed the wonderful aroma that wafted through the door, but scurried quickly past. I would not dare enter that place.

When I came to the corner where I must turn to reach the nursery I saw two Militia officers approaching. They are always in pairs, and the sight of them in their black leather uniforms and the dark shades they all wear sent a tingle of fear through my body. I knew I wasn't breaking any law by being on the street, but they still frightened me and I averted my head as they passed. When I raised my eyes again I caught sight of a figure reflected in a shop window. I saw a strange, brown bat-like creature scuttling along, and realised with a shock that it was my reflection in the glass. No matter how many years pass I have never got used to the image I must now display when I am in the outside world.

The street I was then in had once been a favourite of mine, because many years ago it had some of the best clothing boutiques, a very classy shoe shop, and the wonderful, little cafe where my friends and I would collapse over delicious cups of coffee and rich cakes after a day of retail therapy.

Now it is so boring. There are men's wear shops selling suits and trousers and shirts for men and boys, a shop selling sporting goods and another selling computer equipment. The uniforms worn by the Security Service and Militia officers as well as the overalls worn by the workers are not to be seen in the shops so they must be distributed directly from the factories.

There is one shop selling women's shoes and sandals and lengths of fabric, either wool, cotton or hemp in shades of white or brown. Australia had practically ceased manufacturing clothes by the turn of the century because of the ready availability of cheap clothing from China, Korea and other countries where labour costs were low. Once trade between countries became almost non-existent new factories were built to manufacture clothing material and to make men's clothes. Women are expected to make their own attire from the limited range of fabrics available to them. This is why I looked rather bat-like in the shop window. I learnt how to sew late in life and am not good at it so my brown cloak is not very well made.

On the last corner that I had to cross over, a new mosque has been built. As I passed I admired the curves and lines of the building. Many mosques have been built during the past thirty or so years but also Hindu and Buddhist temples and Jewish synagogues.

Before the influx of migrants from many different countries the Christian religion was already losing support in Australia, and many churches had been sold and converted to houses or unusual restaurants. This decline continued, for most of the newcomers were followers of Buddhism, Islam or Hinduism and Christianity is now a minor religion. Religious beliefs are not, however, a divisive force in our country. The important dividers are wealth and, of course, gender and these elements are crucial in determining ones place in the hierarchical structure of society.

As I was pondering the lessening importance of religion I passed an old hotel. It has been painted up and the "Hotel" sign replaced with one that reads "Accommodation."

After alcohol was banned most of the suburban hotels were turned into dormitory accommodation for the many single men who were required to work in town. More recently they provide family accommodation, for now that the Baby Boomers are getting married and starting families housing is once more at a premium.

The ban on alcohol did not seem to affect the larger, more expensive hotels. They still provide luxury accommodation and first class restaurant service for visiting members of the wealthy elite. I don't know whether or not alcohol is served with meals in these establishments because they are not open to the general public, but it is rumoured that it is.

After passing the hotel and the car park adjoining it I arrived at the nursery. It didn't take me long to find the plants I wanted, and I took them nervously to the counter. Sometimes my shopping card works there, but other times a sale has been refused, and I have had to ask Ali to make a purchase for me.

Today the man behind the counter was friendly and said cheerfully, 'It's a good time to get these in the ground,' as he swiped my card and held out the little machine for me to put in my pin number and code name.

I did this with slightly shaking hands and gave a sigh of relief when the message came up, "Transaction accepted" My hands still shook as he handed me my plants and I felt foolish and angry that a simple transaction could make me feel so nervous.

It was time for me to catch my bus so I returned to the bus stop outside the Centre to wait. As I sat down on the plastic bench the threatening storm broke. Water was soon streaming down the gutter, and a strong wind buffeted the rather fragile bus shelter. For once I was glad to be wearing my badly made cloak with its slightly lop-sided hood because at least I was warm.

When the bus finally arrived I got on. I looked for Corinne amongst the brown-clad passengers, but I couldn't see her so took a seat near the door. I had hoped for a chance to warn her about the Carers, to tell her why we have to be careful about what we say when any of them are near. While we were having afternoon tea she heard Suzie and me talking about Ruth not being at the Centre and asked us why we were so concerned. I had given her an evasive answer because Midge was listening to our conversation. Obviously Corinne is rather naïve and doesn't know what usually happens to widows in our society.

Because the bus had been late it was dark by the time it wound its way up the mountain road and deposited me at my stop. I hadn't thought to put the torch in my bag, so had trouble seeing where I was going as I crossed the road and struggled up my drive. It was such a relief to reach my door and to be safely home again.

My little house felt quite cold so I turned up the heater before I removed the cloak. I was feeling very hungry, as I had only had a cup of tea and a few sandwiches since breakfast. I prepared some vegetables and put a small piece of steak in the pan. At times I don't feel like bothering to prepare a proper meal, but I know I must eat sensibly if I am to remain healthy.

While the meal cooked I thought about dear Ruth. I wished I could ring her up, but she's not on my phone list. Besides Emergency Services and the Civilians' Service Centre, two numbers that I have never rung, my only other phone contacts are Jill, my granddaughters and Ali.

I feel really concerned about Ruth. I know Gerry is ill and that must be why Ruth wasn't at the Centre today. I am frightened about what will happen to her if he should die. Her son defected years ago, and her daughter Phoebe is no longer alive to influence her son-in-law. Without his support she will be killed once she is a lone woman and a family will be moved into her house.

I thought back to those halcyon days of the Mothers' Group when we were all so young and carefree and could keep our children safe. Would we have treasured that time more if we had known how so many of our lives would be shattered?

The evening stretched emptily before me, for there was nothing worth watching on television, and I hadn't been able to find any books I wanted to read among the pitiful little collection at the Centre. My walk through those once familiar streets, and the thought that tomorrow I shall turn eighty, had set me thinking about how the world has changed during my lifetime.

I haven't kept a diary since I was eleven, and then I only put in brief notes like, "went to the beach", or "maths test". My Grandma Mary had given me that diary, and I had never been sure what I should put in it. Now, nearly seventy years later, I have decided to start another diary or perhaps a journal to fill the lonely evening before it's time for bed.

I turned on my computer, opened a new file and commenced to write.

2000

I'm not sure how I should commence this journal. I have no idea if it will ever be read or what the world will be like if or when it is. Will someone get hold of it and think it some sort of fanciful fiction written by an overimaginative old woman? If society has become more Draconian it will probably just be destroyed, but I want to record the changes that occurred to Australian society and how these changes came about.

As a history student I had learnt how rapidly the lives of Afghani women changed during the 1950s when the Taliban retrieved control of their country. Girls who had been receiving an education were once more banned from schools and women lost the freedoms they had gained to dress as they wished and to go out without a male escort and even drive cars. The lives of women in Australia didn't change as rapidly as in this country but they did change just as completely and I want to explain or describe how this came about. I've put the year 2000 at the start of this journal because that was the year I realised from conversations with my Grandma Mary that the lives of Australian women had not always been that great; better than they are now but still not really fair and equal.

At that time I was ten years old and growing up in a household where my parents were equals so this was news to me. Actually I always felt my mother was the more powerful and successful parent. By this I don't mean to imply that my father wasn't a success. He was a lecturer in history at the university and his students loved him but it was my mother who received world-wide accolades as one of the top surgeons in the world.

Grandma Mary was my mother's mother and from her I learnt something of how life had been for women when she was young and how opportunities opened up for them during her lifetime. She saw many changes during her life but subsequent decades since she died have seen the emergence of a radically different society from the one she knew.

How to make sense of what happened to Australian society in just a few short decades? I know the whole world is different now because of climate change, but the earth's physical changes cannot account entirely for what happened to our society. Climate change and the needs for mankind to adapt to what followed in its wake led to a great influx of people into Australia from other countries, but why did we let men with such different attitudes and values take control? The only way I can make sense of what happened is to write down all I lived through in some sort of chronological order and to do this I must go right back to 2000. This was the year when I really got to know my Grandma Mary as a person, and not just a loving presence in my life.

From her I learnt something of what life had been like for women when she was young and how much things changed for women during her lifetime. She told me that during the Second World War many women worked outside the home for the first time during the war years only to be shunted back into becoming housewives once the men returned and took over the jobs they had been doing. At that time, when I was ten, the term housewife had almost disappeared from the language because most women worked outside their homes. There were a few women, like my friend Janine's mother who didn't actually work but she always seemed to be busy doing stuff. No-one would think of her as a housewife.

That summer I was staying with Grandma Mary as I usually did during holidays because my mother was a very busy and important doctor and rarely took a holiday and my father, a university professor, only got a few weeks off each year. Normally I loved being with my grandmother but this summer, for once, my mother had planned to take time off and our little family had been going to go to Surfer's Paradise. At the last minute there had been an explosion in a mine and my mother had flown to the nearest hospital to help treat the men burnt in the blast. I was feeling very cross and hard-done-by and one day I moaned to Grandma about my mother always being so busy.

I was being rather whiny and said miserably, 'I wish I had a mother who didn't work. My friend Janine's mother takes her on holidays every year, and they go shopping or to a film most weekends.'

For once my gentle grandmother looked at me crossly and asked, 'And what does that poor woman do with the rest of her time? She probably fritters it away filling in empty hours shopping for clothes she doesn't need and doing things like yoga or Pilates. You should be proud of your mother. She's one of the best doctors in the country, and has saved hundreds of people from disfigurement with her skills. Anyhow I think every woman should have a chance to work.'

'You told me that you didn't work once you married Grandad', I said rather cheekily.

Two bright red spots appeared on my grandmother's cheeks and she answered sharply, 'No I didn't, but not because I didn't want to. Your grandfather and I both started work as tellers in the same bank. I loved my job and had been promoted to a customer advisory position before he was, but when we married I had to leave work. That was the bank regulation in those days. It was so unfair, but I loved your grandfather very much.' She gave an exasperated sigh and looked pensive. 'I always thought I could go back to work after our children went to school, but by then everything had changed in the banking world and I'd been left behind.'

Feeling a bit mean for upsetting her I said, 'But my uncles and Mum always talk about what a wonderful mother you were, and you're the best grandmother in the whole world.'

'Humph! And your grandfather got to be a bank manager,' she retorted angrily before she turned and left the room.

I sat for a while thinking over our conversation. I hadn't known there had been a time when married women couldn't work and was curious to know why Grandma Mary had married Grandad John if it meant giving up a job she obviously had loved.

My opportunity to ask her about this came a few days later when we were fishing in the creek. It was a lovely summer day, and the sun was shining so brightly on the clear water we could see the fish darting around amongst the rocks. As we stood side by side casting our lines into the water I could see my Grandma Mary relax, so figured it was a good time to bring it up something that had been bugging me.

I said, quite nonchalantly I hoped, 'Why couldn't you keep on working once you got married?

Grandma turned to face me and said abruptly, 'It was the law. Not many places would employ married women, and the banks were particularly strict about that. Men were considered the bread-winners and women in the workforce would be taking jobs away from men'.

'As you liked your job so much why did you marry Grandad when you knew you'd have to give it up? Couldn't you have just lived together, and then you could've still kept on working'?

She looked at me as though I'd suggested something positively evil and said, 'Marion, when we were young, men and women didn't live together before they were married. It just wasn't the done thing. And no decent man would've even suggested that to a respectable woman. No, you either remained a single working woman or you married and gave up your job. Most women accepted that, and quite looked forward to being at home and caring for their husband and then their children. Mind you a lot of women didn't enjoy their jobs, working in shops or factories or offices. They were quite happy to stay at home.'

It was obvious, even to me, that Grandma didn't include herself in that group of contented housewives so I risked quizzing her further by asking, 'Well why weren't you'?

She turned to me, a smile on her face, 'You are a little inquisitor, aren't you? I guess I was just more ambitious than most other girls. I'd completed what is now the equivalent to year ten and would have dearly loved to continue with my studies, perhaps even gone to university. My older brother had, but it was considered a waste of money to educate a girl to that extent as she would just get married and have children. As I told you I started work in a bank and was doing very well, but then I had to leave because I married your grandfather. I suppose it's always rankled with me that I had to give up my job and he went on to become a bank manager, something I could've done. I think in a way I've been a bit unfair because I have held that against him ever since.'

'Is that why you get cross with him at times?'

'No, I don't think so, although it may have made me expect more from him than I would have otherwise. The main way it affected me was that I was determined your mother would have the same opportunities for an education as her two brothers, and that may be why she is such an overachiever now.'

'So you're the reason my mother's such a workaholic Grandma,' I grinned and she slapped me playfully on the behind.

As I read over what I have written I think how in some ways the lives of most women today are somewhat similar to those of the housewives of the fifties and early sixties. Women in Australia are once more housewives, homemakers, servile creatures, unequal partners, whatever you want to call them, but there is a difference. Few girls in the fifties were educated past year ten but this was mainly because higher education was expensive. As the expectation at that time was that most of them would marry at a reasonably early age and begin having children it seemed a waste of money to prepare them for a profession.

The basic difference now is that young women today have been deliberately dumbed down by being given a limited education and deprived of access to anything remotely intellectually stimulating. They also have no freedom to walk outside their homes unaccompanied by a man, have their future husband chosen for them and, unlike the housewives of the fifties who controlled the family budget and were treated as equals in their homes, wives today are subservient in every way. Of course there are some exceptions but these seem to be few.

2010 - 2020

I grew up during the first decade of the new millennium which in retrospect seems like a golden age in which to be young and female in Australia. We received an excellent education, could choose to enter any job or profession we were capable of pursuing and generally relationships between men and women were as equals. Of course there were cases of rape and situations where women suffered at the hands of abusive husbands but generally things were good between the sexes.

I had a happy childhood. Although I sometimes felt neglected by my mother who was always so busy, I had a wonderful relationship with my father. We often went bushwalking and camping together and I really enjoyed the times I spent with him. Although he was quite a few years older than my mother and had a sedentary job he was quite athletic and loved nothing more than being out in the bush. He taught me how to make a fire and cook damper in the ashes, how to catch fish in the little streams we camped beside and how to clean and cook them. At night we'd lie on a ground sheet and look at the inky, star-studded sky while Dad named the various stars and constellations and told me ancient tales connected with their naming. During the days we'd wander through the bush and Dad pointed out which plants were edible and which contained curative properties. We always collected some eucalypt leaves to put in our billy tea and the leaves or berries of mountain pepper trees to add to our meat and vegetable fry-ups.

These times brought us closer together, but also created a certain amount of distance between my mother and me. I felt that if she really wanted to she could take the occasional week off to share these times with us. The little girl who had grumped to Grandma Mary about my mother always being too busy never really went away.

I guess I loved my mother, but there was always an edge to our relationship because I felt she wasn't there enough for me. I was much closer to my father, so it seems natural to follow in his footsteps when it came to choosing my future course of study.

Thinking back to that time when I was deciding what degree course I wished to enrol in reminds me of the glorious holiday I shared with my friend, Janine, before the university year began. Oh, it was so much fun and it will be good to relive it, if only in my memory.

I have finished high school and the long summer break stretches seemingly endlessly before me. I really mean to make the most of these study-free weeks, hanging out with friends and driving around in my new car, a bright yellow Toyota Corolla my parents had given to me for my eighteenth birthday.

As soon as exams finish Janine and I load up the car with tents, sleeping bags, a little gas cooker and various sundry kitchen items, as well as food and clothes and a couple of casks of wine. We have no organised itinerary, but plan to simply go where the mood takes us.

We head up the East Coast, stopping to take photos of each other outside an old-fashioned bakery and standing on rocks on a tiny, crescent-shaped beach feeding quarrelling seagulls the remains of the fish and chips we bought at a takeaway.

After travelling most of the day on a bitumen road we turn onto a gravel track that winds through paddocks and then bushland until we reach a magnificent beach. The day is bright and sunny so we set up our tents, and then go skinny-dipping in the cool, aqua water. We think we have the beach to ourselves so are surprised to see two figures approaching. Giggling inanely we rush to our tents and pull jeans and tee shirt over our wet bodies.

The two guys had been surfing, and their van is parked further along the beach. They tease us, pretending to have seen our naked bodies, and we pretend to be suitably upset. The sun is beginning to set so we make a fire on the beach, open a cask of wine and sit companionably talking and sharing a joint one of the boys has rolled.

Later the boys drive their van back along the track and park near my car, and we cook potatoes in the hot coals and bacon on green twigs we pull from nearby trees. We have sort of paired off, me with Steve, who is tall and blonde, and Janine with Grant, who is shorter but very handsome in a swarthy, Italianate way.

By the time we have finished our belated meal and nearly demolished the cask I am feeling weary and slightly drunk. Steve kisses me passionately and tries to talk me into sharing my tent with him, but I brush him off. Janine spends the night with Grant. Through the thin walls of the tent I hear them giggling, then lots of heavy breathing followed by a long orgasmic scream from Janine. I feel like an eavesdropper and pull my sleeping bag over my head to shut out their noise.

In the morning they say a long and fond goodbye. Steve is barely speaking to me. He is undoubtedly thinking to himself that he'd chosen the wrong girl to go after.

After we say our goodbyes we head back up the track. Janine is all moony about what a wonderful lover Grant had been, but I only half listen to what she says. Although we have been friends since primary school and feel the same way about most things, our attitudes concerning sex are very different.

It isn't that Janine is particularly promiscuous, but she says, 'If it feels right do it.'

I don't want to sound a prude and am certainly no longer a virgin, but I think you should really care about someone if you are going to have sex with them.

At that time we were not to know that in a future society, both of us would be considered 'fallen women' and be locked away by our parents until we could be married off to any old man willing to take us. It's hard to imagine my gentle, loving father or Janine's easy going Dad treating us this way, and some fathers would find it hard, but the alternative was worse. Girls who were not suitably disciplined by their fathers are now removed from their homes, and taken to the Detention Centre. From there they go to one of the houses run by the Madams to become sex slaves to the unmarried members of the Internal Security Force and the Militia.

I know I'm going off on a tangent so will think back to that much lovelier time; back to that summer of youth and freedom.

We spend the rest of that first week mainly exploring the beaches up the coast, then drive into the largest town in the north of the island. The weather has turned chilly so we stay in a caravan park. For the next a couple of days we shop, go to the pictures, eat at rather posh restaurants and visit some of the vineyards in the area before once more continuing our trip around the state.

We travel along the north coast then head inland, passing through beautiful forest country until we reach the plateau, where the landscape is quite bleak in places with stunted, twisted trees, rocky outcrops and sparse undergrowth.

The sun is setting by the time we reach Cradle Valley, and we barely have time to set up our tents before it begins to rain. Fortunately there is a large undercover area equipped with gas barbecues and seating, so we cook steaks and finish off the wine cask before struggling back in the wind and the rain to our tents.

I feel cold all night and hardly sleep because of the wild life prowling around and the sounds of possums fighting and snuffling close by.

This has not been a good introduction to a place we had heard praised so much, but the next day the sun shines and we cook bacon and eggs on our little cooker before heading off for a long walk. We spend several days there, going for different walks each day, cooking our evening meals in the communal area and hanging out with other young travellers.

Amongst this group are a young man and woman who are cycling around the state. Every day they do the longest, hardest walks and sleep at night in tiny silver tents that look a bit like cocoons. There are also two boys, Tom and Frank, who are our age. Like us they are travelling round the state for the first time and they have a station wagon that was Frank's early Christmas present.

Frank plays guitar and Tom a mouth organ. Celia, the girl half of the cycling couple, plays the flute, so our evenings are spent singing or just listening to the music these three make. Often the evenings end with a beautifully haunting solo from Celia that blends with the sighing of the wind through the encroaching forest. We all wander back to our tents feeling uplifted and at peace.

After leaving Cradle Valley we drive down the West Coast, which is beautiful and rugged, and into the mining town renowned in the past for its pink, bare hills that in times past must have looked like something you would see on the moon. Changes in mining practises have resulted in some of the trees returning, but it still looks quite spectacular.

From there we drive down to the little fishing and tourist village that is the starting point for trips up the famed Gordon River. As the weather has turned nasty we again hire a caravan and the next day make the boat trip up the river. When we arrive at the spot in the river where the boat turn round there are four canoeists waiting to hitch a ride back. Two of them are girls, and Janine and I talk to them during the return journey. Their canoeing trip sounds so exciting we decide we will do that trip during our next vacation.

By that time we are running out of money so the next day we drive home, feeling satisfied that we have almost circled our island state.

If I have spent an overly long time back in the past recounting this journey it's because I was enjoying so much reliving that joyous time but I also wanted to show what freedom we had in those days compared with the lives of the young girls today. None of them will ever drive a car, ride a bicycle or paddle a canoe or even hike in the bush. None of them will know what it was like to meet and talk with boys and men as equals. They have lost the right to all these experiences.

On that sad note I will end this entry for today.

2009 - 2011

By the time Janine and I return from our trip around the island exam results are out and I have matriculated with an excellent score.

My mother says proudly, 'With those marks you could get into Medicine.'

There is no way I want to emulate my mother's life. It seems to me to be one of unremitting work and worry. Instead I enrol to do a Bachelor of Arts Degree, majoring in History and English, and plan to either lecture at university, like my father, or teach at a matriculation college.

University life is great. I have lots of friends, both boys and girls, enjoy the study and get good results. My one disappointment with regard to university life is that the political fire I had expected from my fellow students is missing.

I had read about the Anti-Conscription protests and the Vietnam War Moratoriums held by students throughout Australia during the latter part of the sixties and the early seventies. On a local level there had been the numerous protests staged against the damning of the Franklin River during the eighties, and university students had been avid participants in those protests. I had thought there would now be protesting against Australia's treatment of the so-called 'boat people', who are really only people fleeing intolerable conditions in their own lands, but nothing seems to fire up my fellow students.

During my third year at university there are things going on in our country that I find appalling, and I expect everyone to feel as I do. There are hundreds of refugees living under wretched conditions in off-shore detention centres and this has been going on for years. There are reports in the papers of inmates committing suicide by swallowing razor blades, of women and children being raped, of hunger strikes and of the psychological damage being done to these people by the long years of incarceration.

All this year I feel angry at the way this government is treating the refugees, and disappointed that none of my friends seem to share my concerns. When I voice them I get answers like, 'Well they were trying to jump the queue', or 'The Indonesians are to blame. They send them off from there in rotten boats.'

There also seems to be little concern about climate change amongst my fellow students, and these are intelligent people who should care. Polar ice is melting, the world experiences more violent storms and there is severe drought in some countries and record flooding in others. Already sea levels have risen and low lying island communities have been displaced to any country that will take them. When I say to my friends that politicians throughout the world should be combining to halt any further damage to our planet they just shrug and say annoying things like, 'We can't rely on renewable power sources yet', and 'The scientists are just panicking'. Most annoying of all are the ones who try and convince me we are just in another climate cycle and that the world has always had periods of cooling and heating. I feel like throttling these climate sceptics and wonder how they managed to get into university when they are so stupid.

At least my father shares my concerns about climate change and we discuss what should be being done to at least attempt saving our planet. We also have wonderful discussions about many of the works I am studying and I actually enrol in his unit on The Age of Revolution. Unlike most male historians who seem to concentrate their lectures on wars, weapons and the economy my father's lectures are about people. I am charmed, as are most of his other students, by the way in which he brings to life how ordinary people lived and felt. My father is a brilliant and popular lecturer and we become even closer during my university years.

My mother and I spend very little time together. She always seems to come home late during the week, and stays in bed until noon on Saturdays. On Sundays she makes a point of cooking a roast dinner in the middle of the day, usually lamb with mint sauce and baked vegetables. Shades of the meals her mother cooked for her and their family so long ago.

When she has the time she is a good cook and also a relaxed hostess. She encourages me to invite friends to these dinners, and often I have my current boyfriend over to share them with us. Mum always charms them totally with her blonde beauty, total efficiency in the kitchen and interesting conversation.

After meeting my mother friends say things like, 'You must be so proud of her,' and, 'Your mother's so easy to talk to. When you're with her it's hard to believe she's so famous.'

I mumble some gauche reply, agreeing with them, but I continue to resent her absorption in her work even though I know this is childish.

In September of my final year at university my beloved Grandma Mary dies suddenly of a heart attack. No one had even known there was any problem with her heart so it is a terrible shock. The funeral is ghastly with Mum dry-eyed and stoical and me blubbing like a baby. Grandad John stumbles into the church supported by Mum's brother, my uncle Tim and his wife Mellissa. Afterwards they take him home with them, and care for him for the remaining few years of his life.

I am amazed when my mother goes back to work the day after the funeral, for I am still feeling so sad and bereft I can't even bother opening a book.

When my mother returns from the hospital I tell I can't understand how she can act as if nothing has happened.

She looks at me with those blue eyes that can turn a steely grey and says, 'that's because you don't have work you must do, or people depending on you to do it.'

Later she apologises for being so short with me and we hug, but her remark has stung, has made me feel she thinks I am wasting my time with further study.

Originally I was planning to continue studying; had even decided I would do my doctorate on the relationships between men and women as depicted in early Australian fiction. Now, stirred on by my mother's barb about not having work I must do, I decide to apply for a position teaching English at one of the new matriculation colleges and am successful.

2012 – 2030

Firthside Matriculation College is only a few years old, and was built to cater for the increasing numbers of students who are staying on until year twelve. At this time unemployment isn't as high as it was to become, but employers can be choosy, and many are demanding higher levels of education from the young people who they employ

Before the school year commences there is a week of staff meetings when we meet our department heads, discuss the curriculum to be followed and are allocated classes. There is a nice atmosphere about the place. Everyone is welcoming and friendly, and all staff members meet for morning, lunch and afternoon breaks in the big, modern staffroom.

At the beginning of the week people are inclined to stay in groups that relate to the department in which they teach. By the middle of the week there is some mixing, but I don't meet Bill until Friday.

Of course I noticed him the very first day, even though I was busy getting to know the other teachers in my group. The Maths/Science teachers congregated at the opposite end of the long room from where we English teachers were.

There had been a hoot of laughter and I looked across. In the middle of the laughing group was one of the handsomest men I had ever seen. He was tall and broad-shouldered, and his thick blonde hair glinted in the sun that shone in from a nearby window. As I stared he turned my way and looked at me with smiling blue eyes. My heart did a flip, and I determined I would make an opportunity to get to know this man as soon as possible.

On the final day of orientation week it is decided we will all go to the pub over the road for lunch. I am walking across with June, who has been teaching at the college since it opened, and Phyllis, who is a new recruit like me.

Bill comes alongside me and says in a deep, laughing voice, 'Hi June. Are you going to introduce me to your new compatriots?'

June makes the introductions. When we reach the pub Bill stays at my side, and makes sure we are seated next to each other at the long table that has been reserved for our group.

It is a long, boozy lunch. We have all worked hard during the week, but next week the real work will begin. I think everyone feels this is like an oasis, a time to relax and let down their hair. Some people begin telling quite corny jokes, but we laugh at them anyway. Three of the science teachers have a sculling competition, egged on by the rest of us.

As the lunch progresses an almost childish atmosphere takes over. We are like kids let out to play. I guess we all feel this is the last time we will have together for a while when we are not hiding behind the serious personas of teachers. Perhaps there is a bit of the child remaining in all who follow our profession, and this may be what leads us into it.

Bill and I talk the afternoon away. Gradually people leave, some to cook meals for husbands or to pick up children from grandparents or day care, others to go home to empty flats or dependent parents. We are the last to leave and have drunk far too much to drive ourselves home so we share a taxi and promise, between drunken kisses, to meet the next day when we return to retrieve our cars.

This is the beginning of our love affair, and during that year we spend every possible moment together. I stay at his flat every weekend and at least a couple of nights through the week. On the evenings when work or other commitments mean we can't be together we ring each other before going to bed, and have long, loving conversations. He is everything I ever wanted in a man, intelligent, caring, handsome and sexy.

Because teachers are meant to set a good example, relationships between staff members are rather frowned on, so we keep our love a secret for most of the year. In a way this adds piquancy to our affair because we pretend to be merely friends while in the presence of our work mates, but sneak the odd kiss when no one is around.

At the end of that year Bill proposes and gives me a beautiful diamond and sapphire engagement ring. On the last day of term the staff members put on a lunch for us and give us an exquisitely hand-painted, stoneware dinner set. There is quite a bit of hilarity about us not having to sneak around any longer as Bill is going to make an honest woman of me. Obviously our pretence hasn't been as convincing as we thought.

During the long Christmas break we plan our wedding that is to take place during the first term vacation. We also begin house hunting.

Bill has an inheritance from a maiden aunt, and together with what he has saved during the four years he's been teaching there is enough for a deposit on a reasonable house. We have decided we need something big because we both want a large family. Like me Bill was an only child, and we want our children to grow up with siblings, and not be "lonely onlys" as we had been.

We spend many days looking at dozens of houses but finally we find the one that suits us. It is a weatherboard bungalow style house, built sometime in the seventies, so is about fifty years old. Despite its age it has been well maintained outside and has beautiful established gardens with some really lovely trees and a huge back yard. The kitchen and bathrooms need upgrading and in several rooms the paintwork is decidedly shabby, but it has a lovely big lounge room, a second entertaining area and four bedrooms. We sign on the spot and spend the remainder of the holidays planning the kitchen upgrade and painting walls.

Things change a bit between Mum and me during the months leading up to the wedding. She must have told the hospital she needed some time off because she is certainly more available during this time. She comes with me when I choose my dress, helps with the guest list and organises the reception. She also puts on a great pre-wedding party attended by all my friends as well as Bill's widowed mother, Alice. I have met her a few times during the past year and know what a shy, retiring woman she is, but Mum charms her completely.

Our wedding day is the most wonderful of my life. After the reception we spend the night in our house. In the morning I disentangle myself from Bill's arms and then just sit, watching him sleep, admiring his handsome face and thinking how much I love him.

We have a brief honeymoon travelling around the state, visiting some of the spots I had been to years before in my little yellow Toyota.

Neither of us has been out of Australia so we plan to have an overseas holiday at a later date as a sort of belated honeymoon. There is unrest in many parts of the world.

Terrorist groups have been plaguing our world now for over twenty years but no sooner is one group brought under control than another appears. The current rash of terrorists seem to strike randomly and there have been bombings of trains and buses in England, Spain and France as well as in many Middle Eastern countries. We decide to wait until things settle down a bit before venturing out of our country, but something happens to makes me doubt if I will ever travel.

Only a few months after Bill and I married there is a terrorist attack in Bali. My mother flies there to treat burns patients after bombs are exploded at two popular hotels. Many of the injured are Australian tourists, and she has gone with a team of medics to treat the injured and organise the return of others to our country. Shortly after take-off for the return journey to Australia the plane carrying the medical team and some of their patients explodes killing all on board. Because the black box is never found the cause of the explosion remains unknown, but the general consensus is that terrorists were responsible.

After the many years of feeling unimportant in my mother's life we had become closer during the months leading up to the wedding and I had hoped this would continue. Now she is gone I grieve for her, and wish so much we could have had many more years together. I regret that I had hung onto my childish jealousy and feelings of neglect; had failed to understand that it wasn't lack of love for me, but her overwhelming sense of responsibility to her patients that kept her absent from my life.

While I am sad and full of regrets after my mother's death, my father is devastated. He changes from a relatively vital, active man to a shambling wreck. He takes a year's sabbatical from the university, but does little work on the book he had been writing about the French Revolution. Often when I drop in to see him on my way home from college he is sitting staring into space, a lost look in his eyes. Although the housekeeper continues to cook an evening meal for him I know most of it is finishing up in the bin. He has always been a trim, fit-looking man, but now he is becoming almost skeletal. I have to do something to drag him out of his depression.

I had continued to toy with the idea of writing about the relationships between men and women as depicted in early Australian literature. He appears to have lost interest in the French Revolution so I suggest to him that we could combine, with him writing about the factual aspects of life for pioneering men and women, and me writing about the fictional portrayals.

He brightens up at the prospect of us working together and gradually becomes less despondent. I actually don't ever complete my part of the book but Dad is soon completely engrossed in researching the topic. He begins taking trips to Sydney and Canberra, and even some small country towns where local history rooms hold the primary sources he needs. He gathers together copies of letters, bills of sale and household account books written by frugal housewives in beautiful copperplate or childish printing. Now when I drop in to see him he greets me with a boyish look on his face, and shares his finds with me.

He shows me an entry from one of the account books and says in amazement, 'Look at this. Samuel Jones bought his wife a sewing machine before they even had a plough.'

Another time he has a sheaf of letters that had been the correspondence between an early settler Bill Green and his wife Amy. They are written on scrappy pieces of paper and the spelling is atrocious but as Dad says, 'You can feel the love and respect that existed between those two.'

My father had always been interested in how the lives of ordinary people were affected by momentous historical events. Through his research he gains a fresh insight into the lives of the early Australian settlers, both those who had come as free men and women and as convicts.

One day he says, 'You know we've been told so much about the mateship between Australian men in the bush, but it was also there between the husbands and wives. Their lives were hard, but they worked together as a team. That was the only way they survived in, what was for most of them, a totally different kind of life in a strange new land.'

Thinking of this makes me think how any semblance of "mateship" no longer exists between Australian men and women. Remembering the lives of my mother and grandmother, and indeed my own, it appears as though women have for centuries been fighting an unfairly weighted battle to gain some semblance of equality. It seems they have it for a while only to have it taken away again.

But I digress and must go back to that time.

Eventually Dad finishes his book, without any input from me. It becomes a best seller as well as being used as a university textbook in both Australian History and Women's Studies for many years until it is banned along with any books that depicted women in a favourable light and as active partners with men.

Working on that book has given my father an interest in living again, and he even returns to part-time lecturing.

Although I had intended to work with Dad on the book, teaching, preparation and marking take up a lot of my time. I want to spend all my time away from work with Bill for we both treasure the weekends. Sometimes we go bushwalking or camping or shout ourselves a time away at some luxury resort. These escape weekends are unusual though for most of the time we just hang out, shopping at the market, doing the household chores and going out to see a film or play or to dinner with friends. Sundays are generally our day for lying in bed, making love until the afternoon then cooking up feasts together and dining in style with a bottle of good red wine.

Bill and I both want children, but originally decided we would wait and have at least two years together just as a couple, to have fun and to travel.

For some strange reason losing my mother has an unexpected effect on me. I begin to feel quite clucky, find myself peering at babies in prams and pausing to look in the windows of baby shops at the cute and tiny clothes on display. Perhaps I am simply responding to some biological instinct; some need to replace one loved relative with another in the only possible way I can. Having lost both my beloved Grandma Mary and my mother I am the only living female of my line. This may be the reason why I now badly want a child.

When I tell Bill about the way I am feeling he says, 'You know how I feel. I want us to have lots of kids. At present it's hard to know where it'd be safe to travel to, so why don't we start our family now? We can always take them with us when this mad rash of terrorist activity has stopped.'

During the next year I conceive twice only to miscarry at three months. The doctor says I should be able to carry a baby to full term, but it would be wise to wait a while before trying again to allow my body to recover completely. I am distraught and feel a complete failure as a woman.

After the second miscarriage I remember my grandmother telling me my mother had miscarried twice, and that was why I was an only child. I had undoubtedly been grumping about feeling unwanted. She'd told me my mother didn't talk about that time because she had felt such a failure. Obviously we share some biological weakness. The thought that she would have understood completely just how I am feeling now makes me miss her anew, and feel even more depressed.

To help me get over my depression Bill suggests we plan a trip overseas, and looking at Lonely Planets and poring over maps certainly cheers me up. We toss-up between going to Italy or France, but there has been some rioting in Paris and other French cities so we decide to explore Italy.

We fly to Rome and have a wonderful week exploring that ancient city. Coming from a country that in terms of white settlement is still very young we are fascinated to discover ancient pieces of wall and fragments of statuary hidden away in unexpected places around the city. It makes us realise how new and raw our Australian civilization is.

After that week we hire a tiny Italian car and travel around the glorious countryside, stopping at quaint little villages and often sleeping in primitive accommodation. We eat and drink what the locals are having and acquire a love of good, strong coffee, fresh pasta and rich, garlicky tomato sauce.

During the year after our lovely holiday in Italy I become pregnant once more. Bill cossets me as though I am a porcelain doll. When I pass the dreaded three-month mark he takes me out to dinner at the most expensive restaurant in town to celebrate. He drinks champagne and I have soda water, but we both end the evening equally tipsy on happiness.

Our beautiful Fiona is born on June 2016. She has a mass of dark hair and my brown eyes. When I hold her in my arms for the first time I feel the most wonderful sense of completion, as well as the most overwhelming one of love.

A few days later, when the baby blues kick in, I feel sad that neither my mother nor grandmother is here to share this time with me. I cry on and off all one day, but the nurses say this is quite usual and are very kind. When Bill sees my sad face he rushes out and comes back with his arms full of flowers and a pink plastic heart on a stick. He looks so funny and awkward I begin to laugh and then feel much better.

With the birth of our daughter I gain several new friends, thanks to the district nurse who organises our mothers' group. We are all first time mothers, living in the same suburb, and she brings us together so that we can support each other during the first, often testing months of motherhood.

Soon we have become very close and meet once a week at each other's homes. As our babies grow we go as a group to parks and playgrounds. When our babies are old enough we take them to the pool and teach them to swim under the guidance of an instructor.

This is such a joyous year as well as a year of change in the relationship between Bill and me. Being parents somehow increases our depth of feeling for each other.

Besides being a year of change for us it is also an important one for our country. We have a change of government in the November elections and the Labor Party comes to power under the leadership of Geoffrey Curtis.

We are both pleased with Labor's win, but although they had promised much little change occurs during the years they are in power. Australia manages to survive a global financial crisis in a strong position, more as a result of a strong banking sector that from political manoeuvring, but illegal immigration continues to be a problem and no strong action is achieved regarding climate change.

To make up for the hard line they are taking regarding illegal refugees, who continue to arrive in old and leaky boats, the Labor party increases the quota for legal immigrants and supports family reunions. They also work hard at getting the unemployed back into the workforce, and improve the number and quality of childcare facilities to enable mothers to return to work.

Bill and I had hoped for more from this government and are disappointed with their performance. Like many of our friends we are concerned about the lack of action both in Australia and many other countries regarding climate change.

Although we consider ourselves politically aware, and talk with friends about the plight of refugees and the need for something to be done to halt global warming we just talk. We take no active part in protests or campaigns, for we are more concerned with our little family and the life we are making together.

Two years after Fiona was born I give birth to another baby girl who we name Jill. She is blonde and blue-eyed, a miniature version of my mother.

From the start Fiona had been an active, noisy baby, full of energy and mischief. In contrast Jill is quiet and gentle and less adventurous than her older sister. Looking back it seems that from the time they were babies I could tell the sort of women they would grow up to be.

Many of my friends in the mothers' group have had a second baby at about the same time as I, and we continue to meet on a regular basis. For the children it is almost like having a whole lot of cousins, and this is great for them. Like me, many of the mothers were only children. Others have family in a different state so the mothers' group gives us all a kind of extended, replacement family.

Despite this supportive network, by the time Jill is two I begin to think about returning to work. I had been determined to be unlike my mother, and to put my children ahead of work, but I have come to see that I won't be happy living as my grandmother had. Although I adore my girls, I have spent four years at home and am beginning to feel the need of more mental stimulation and adult company. Fiona is already attending a very good childcare centre four mornings a week and Jill is keen to join her sister there.

The Curtis Government has funded extra childcare centres in all major towns and cities. These centres all have trained staff members, excellent facilities and commercial kitchens that provide the children with a hot, nourishing meal at midday. If you place an order in the morning they can also supply the evening meal for parents to take away with them when they collect their children. This is a popular option for weary parents, and lessens the consumption of unhealthy fast foods in families where both parents work.

Because Bill and I teach at the same school we always go to the centre together after work. Sometimes we order our dinner in the morning and pick it up when we collect the girls, but more often we don't bother. When we get home it is usually still quite early so one of us bathes the girls while the other cooks the meal. After dinner we play with the girls or read to them until it is their bedtime.

Saturdays are usually spent catching up with household and gardening chores and about once a month we have our mothers' group outings. Sundays are our special family days when just we four do things together.

I suppose this all sounds rather mundane and unexciting, but we both enjoyed our jobs, the girls were dear happy little people to be around and we loved each other very much.

Compared with the marriages I see now ours was a sharing of life by two equals. Either one of us could bathe the babes, cook the dinner, put on a load of washing or clean the toilets. We never argued about who should do what, but worked together as a partnership.

Bill didn't live long enough to see the greatest changes in male/female relationships that have taken place. As I relive that time I wonder what he would make of this world where men dominate their wives and the women behave like handmaidens to their husbands. Would he have changed as so many other men did?

When we were first married we at times had slightly kinky sex where he was sort of dominating. At times when I took his penis into my mouth he held my head down and said, 'Service me wench.' Other times he tied my hands and feet to the bed with scarves and touched me everywhere until I was so frantically aroused I begged him to enter me. We stopped playing those games when I was pregnant with Fiona and never went back to them, but perhaps they were an indication of his desire to dominate me that he kept hidden. Would it have resurfaced when the world changed and it became the norm for men to subjugate their women? Somehow I don't think so.

Now back to the past.

Many of the other mothers also return to work at about the same time as I. We still meet as a group some Saturdays. These become big events because our husbands now join us for barbecues in the parks or picnics at the beach. The children play happily together with the men supervising, while we women catch up on what is going on in each other's lives.

We talk about our jobs and changes that are occurring in our working environments. We also discuss plays or films we have seen and books we have read. We talk about our children, of course, but we share other interests.

In 2022 an election is called and Bill and I both hope the Curtis Government will be re-elected because their major platform at this election is climate change and the need to invest in clean forms of power generation. We have hopes that during a second term they will finally get things happening in this area.

We hold an election party at our place. We invite some of the teachers with whom we work, as well as our friends from the mothers' group. It is a big noisy affair with much talk about climate change, which is of concern to many of us. Most of us are dyed-in-the-wool Labor voters, and if there are any among us who vote for the conservatives they keep their preferences to themselves.

Bill has invited Assad who has been teaching with him in the maths/science department since the beginning of the year. Assad brings his beautiful wife Tahani with him to the party. She and their two boys arrived in Australia from Saudi Arabia the previous month and I have only met her once before. On this night she seems overwhelmed by what she is seeing, so I join her on the couch where she is sitting and ask her how she is settling in.

She looks at me with her great, dark luminous eyes and says, 'It is all so strange to me. Not only to see men and women talk and laugh and drink together, but also the idea of the people being able to choose who will lead them. This does not happen in my country and the concept is hard for me to adjust to.'

She looks lost and bewildered and I would like to continue our conversation, but just then someone turns the sound up on the television and this puts a damper on all conversations in the room. Everyone crowds round the T.V. set, and when it becomes apparent the Curtis Government has been returned with a reasonable majority we all cheer.

During the next few months Bill and I try to draw Assad and Tahani into our social group. Their sons are roughly the same ages as our daughters, and we think it would be good for both the parents and the children to share our typical Aussie barbecues and picnics.

Unfortunately this does not work out. Although Assad makes friends with the other men and their children play happily with the rest of the kids it is obviously more difficult for Tahani. She sits silently while we females yammer on about our jobs or politics or the environment, and I can tell she feels uncomfortable.

She is also not at ease when the men join us, and pulls her headscarf around her chin and keeps her eyes lowered while they are around. The men all think she is gorgeous, but she is unapproachable and they don't know how to take her.

On one occasion Gerry, who is tall, handsome and the group flirt steps out of line with her. He is forever giving one of us a hug and saying how beautiful we all look. We joke about his behaviour and his long-suffering wife, Ruth, is always offering him to anyone who will take him off her hands. We are all used to his behaviour and accept it as light-hearted foolery, but when he puts his arm around Tahani she pulls away as though horrified. Assad steps forward, a threatening look on his face, and for a moment I fear things may get ugly. Fortunately Gerry sees quickly that he has offended and makes a hurried apology, but it is an uncomfortable moment.

Tahani also finds it difficult to understand the way we women talk about our husbands, how we sometimes criticize things they do.

One day when the men seem to be taking an inordinately long time to cook the barbecue I call out to them, 'What're you boys doing? The kids are starving.'

Tahani looks at me, a slightly horrified on her beautiful face, and says, 'Why do you call them boys? In my country the servants are called boys.'

Someone says, 'Well they're our servants today,' and we all joke about this while she looks on bewildered.

She always wears full-length, floaty gowns and matching headscarves that conceal everything but her lovely, exotic face with its high-cheekbones and dark eyes. She sits there so still and serene while the rest of us cavort around in our shorts and tee shirts. I look at the cellulite on Toni's legs, the baby bulge Jill has never lost and at my own tanned but freckled arms and legs and try to see how we must appear to her. She makes the rest of us women feel gauche and ungraceful just by being herself. Perhaps because of this we don't make enough effort to draw her out and get to know her.

In time she and Assad no longer join our group at these social events but Bill and Assad remain good friends at work. At first I worry that we have not made her feel welcome enough and that she will be lonely. When I voice these concerns to Bill he says two of her sisters are coming soon from Saudi Arabia with their husbands and children. They are immigrating to Australia under the Family Reunion Plan, and he is sure she will be happier once they arrive.

On the political front the Labor government has finally brought in a carbon tax, a belated first step in the fight to halt climate change. The Liberals adamantly reject this measure and opt instead for assisting the polluting industries to become cleaner. They run a strong fear campaign against the tax and convince many that it is resulting in an unnecessary increase in the cost of power, food and petrol.

Other problems bug the Labor party and when Liberals block supply following the 2024 budget a double dissolution follows and another election is held. Unfortunately this results in a resounding victory for the Liberals.

Once in power they are faced with implementing their policies regarding climate change, and the realisation that these won't cut greenhouse levels quickly enough to satisfy the world body that has been set up to monitor the levels of carbon pollution of all countries. They now set about encouraging wealthy investors from other countries to immigrate to Australia and set up alternative energy industries.

Soon Australia is being flooded with immigrants from China and India where overcrowding and pollution is making life difficult as well as from the wealthy oil rich countries, in particular from Saudi Arabia. The ever-increasing price of petrol has made this country exceedingly wealthy, and they are looking for long-term investments.

We also begin accepting refugees from some of the small island nations whose lives are already being affected by sea level rise, but the harsh policies towards so-called boat people continue. The politicians call them "queue jumpers" and continue to turn the boats around or process the refugees on offshore islands. Eventually the increase in the cost of travel and the strengthening of our border security puts a stop to this trade in human lives.

Even without these so-called illegal refugees our population increases from twenty three million to close to thirty in the space of a few years, and this rapid increase puts pressure on employment and housing as well as health and education services.

By 2028, when an election is called, ways of dealing with these problems are the voter's main concerns, as well as a general call for a change to the immigration policy.

Of interest to Bill and me are the problems in the education system. Schools are overcrowded and class sizes have doubled, thus increasing the stress experienced by teaching staff. Surveys show that boys are under-performing in all grades, from prep to matriculation, and that they exhibit significantly more behavioural problems in the overcrowded classrooms than girls. It is becoming increasingly obvious boys are trailing the girls under the current education system. Through testing it is determined boys and girls learn in different ways, and it is thought both sexes would benefit from being in separate classes.

Bill and I initially opt for the trialling of segregated schooling for boys and girls; for we are convinced by the testing it could be beneficial to both genders. We are happy for Fiona and Jill to attend an all-girl high school. Many of our fellow teachers and most parents with sons are eager to see segregation trialled for there is real concern about the lack of academic success of so many boys and the fact that girls far outnumber the boys at all the universities. Segregated learning seemed to be a logical step.

If any of us could have envisioned where it would lead we wouldn't have been so keen. The present situation shows what can happen to a good idea when those in power have a hidden agenda.

During the run up to the 2028 election education is one of the principle platforms, with the Curtis opposition promising extra funding for education with particular emphasis on adult migrants.

In contrast the Liberals tout that the current funding is sufficient but not being used for optimum results. Their platform is that there should be suitable educational opportunities for all, and current practices are having a detrimental effect with regard to the education of males.

The first time I really become aware of Mohamed Raman is a few months before the election, when he visits our school. He is a cousin of Assad and had arrived in Australia a couple of years after his relative. Like Assad he is also a teacher, but he is very interested in politics. He joined the

Liberal Party and campaigned actively for them during the 2024 election. He is now standing in the upcoming federal election, and as part of his campaign visiting many schools in the state to talk to teachers about his party's stand with regard to education.

When he walks into the classroom in which our meeting with him is to be held we female staff members let out an audible sigh.

He wears a beautifully tailored, dark grey suit and a brilliantly white shirt. His hair is black and curly, he has skin the colour and sheen of polished blackwood, and his eyes are so dark they seem to glisten. No wonder we all sigh at the sight of him.

Our principle introduces him and he stands before us, a man totally at ease with himself. He speaks with a slight English accent and his speech, though short, is intimate and sincere. He outlines some the changes his government will make to the education system if they are re- elected.

He begins with what is to become the catch cry of the Liberals and later the New Australia Party; 'We are concerned with providing a suitable education for each and every child.'

He then goes on to say that he wants the best possible education for all children; one that will prepare them for their adult lives.

He criticises the current policy whereby all children are being educated to matriculation level, and says that he understands that we are bearing the brunt of the Labor Party's policy of extending the school leaving age to eighteen. Because of this policy we have to cope with the presence of disinterested students in overcrowded classrooms.

He says the Liberals plan to change this. They will build vocational colleges in all cities and major towns. Here the less academic students will receive a suitable education, one that will prepare them for employment in the trades and service industries.

He finishes by saying that once more the matriculation colleges will regain their original purpose – that of educating the brightest students and preparing them for higher education and their future roles in the professions.

We all cheer and clap. Here is a politician who understands the problems we face every day because of the previous government's policy of extending the school leaving age. Under this new plan we will no longer have to cope with unwilling and incompetent students who are just filling in time until they turn eighteen.

While he is talking to our group it occurs to me that Mohamed Raman resembles Osama Bin Laden, the Afghani rebel who appeared on our television sets at the beginning of the millennium. Osama had been infamous for having masterminded the bombing of the twin towers in New York. Mohamed is much younger and clean-shaven, but he has the same hypnotic gaze as that rebel leader and the same charismatic power.

After his talk, which has been held in one of the classrooms, we all move to the staff room for tea and cake. Mohamed circulates around the room balancing his teacup elegantly in his large, brown hand. Bill and I are standing together when the principal introduced us, adding the information that I teach English and Bill teaches Maths.

What strikes me is that Bill, who is very tall and handsome, seems diminished in the presence of this man. Although he is no taller than Bill, Mohamed stands so erectly he seems to tower over every man in the room, including my husband.

He asks us if there is a gender bias in our classes and I laughingly reply, 'Well for years there was a strong element of self-regulated segregation, but this is no longer the case.'

Bill interjects, 'Yes, Marion and I used to joke about her girls and my boys but the pendulum's shifted. Now girls make up more than fifty percent of my maths classes, and the science teachers have noticed the same trend.'

I join in, 'And I have more boys studying English than previously was the case. Mind you many of them are not the least bit interested in reading novels or analysing a poem, but for some ridiculous reason they need matriculation English to get into many of the trades. I like your idea of increasing the number of vocational colleges. I'm sure some of my lumpish boys would be better off studying subjects more relevant to their future working lives.'

At that moment the principal joins us and leads our guest off for further introductions, but before leaving Mohamed shakes hands with both of us and thanks us for our input. I feel a small frisson of excitement as he briefly holds my hand.

After he leaves some of us stay behind discussing the visit. The way in which he has talked about the importance of education has made us all feel that we teachers are at the forefront of making our nation great. Even though he is standing for the wrong party, as far as many of us are concerned, we are all impressed by him and by his sincerity.

That night as we are undressing for bed I say to Bill, 'Wasn't it great to meet a politician who really understands our problems and what we have to put up with?'

Bill answers slowly, 'Yes he certainly seems to know what he's talking about, but there's something I don't quite trust about the fellow.'

'I thought he was marvellous and very sincere. And he's been a teacher and he's also a parent so his concerns about education are genuine. Whatever could you not trust?'

'I don't know. I can't put my finger on it, but there's something about him that bothers me.'

I laugh, 'It couldn't be that he is unbelievably good-looking and had every female in the room drooling?'

'Including you,' Bill retorts, but then continues, 'No it's not that. There was something about the way he talked about "suitable education". It set some alarm bells ringing and I'm not sure why. I think his ideas of a suitable education for all could be rather elitist and different from ours.'

I don't see it this way and think Bill is simply showing a bit of male jealousy or insecurity, so reassure him by being especially loving towards him when we are in bed.

During this campaign, while education is important, the major platform on which the election is fought is immigration.

Because of the very open immigration policies of both the Labor and Liberal Governments the rapid population increase has created problems although Liberals insist the advantages outweigh the disadvantages. They point to the huge advancements that had taken place in industry during their four years in power. They are convinced this growth will lead to ever increasing work opportunities, and that meanwhile the country can afford to provide for those unable to get jobs.

In contrast the opposition emphasises that there are increasing numbers of unemployed people particularly amongst those less educated. They want to see a tightening up of the immigration policy, and strict controls put in place to determine eligibility based on educational or financial criteria.

Many of the newcomers have come from Saudi Arabia, where there has been little industrial or technological development. The Saudis see Australia as a country in which they can invest some of the enormous wealth they are accruing as oil supplies became scarcer and therefore more expensive. The majority of these migrants obtain work in family businesses and the professions. Most of them are already fluent in English because a lot of the males have been educated in America or England.

There are also a large number of wealthy Chinese and Indian migrants many of whose children are attending universities in Australia. The overcrowding and pollution in their homelands has meant that these students have wanted to stay. Once the Australian government begins inviting the wealthy from all nations to invest in Australia with citizenship on offer as encouragement the parents join their student children and make Australia their new home.

Another large group of migrants consist of those from the low-lying islands in the Pacific who have sought sanctuary in Australia when their lands were inundated by rising sea levels. Most of this group speak little or no English and have received a limited education. They fill lowly paid, menial positions or remain unemployed. Often their children are disadvantaged at school and have problems fitting into an alien culture.

Of course the assimilation of all these very diverse groups into the existing Australian culture creates problems, but they do not seem to be insurmountable.

On the evening of the 2028 election Bill and I once more host a big party for our friends and workmates. Although most of our guests are the same as on the previous occasions this year the dynamics are different. Many of our acquaintances have become disillusioned with both major parties, particularly some of the women from the mothers' group. While none of our group has experienced employment problems, our children are now all attending school and the rapid population growth has put a strain on the education system.

I join my friends from the mothers' group just as Toni is saying, 'I don't care how much they say they are spending on education it obviously isn't enough.'

Ruth, who besides being a mother is a teacher at the local primary school, agrees, 'Of course it isn't. I have forty-five children in my class and a quarter of them need special English lessons. I only get a specialist teacher to help them for five hours a week, and that's not nearly enough. I feel sorry for the poor little things, but there's not a lot I can do for them. With so many other kids to teach, these migrant kids misbehave, especially some of the boys.'

Sara, another of the mothers joins in, 'My Josie is getting so she doesn't want to go to school because there is so much bullying in the playground. I think the Libs have got it right with their plans to extend the trialling of segregated schools Quite frankly I would be very happy to see both of my girls in a single-sex school.'

Listening to these concerned parents makes me think of the Liberal's policy as espoused by Mohamed of providing a suitable education for all children, and to wonder how many of our guests have changed their political allegiances in this election.

Once the results start coming in it is obvious to all of us in the room that Liberals have retained power, but with a reduced majority. Mohamed Raman has polled well and secured a seat in the Liberal Party, as have several other newcomers to our country. Our celebrations at that election eve party are much lower key than in previous years for I think, like me, most of our friends think neither major party knows how they should lead us.

During the following year the Liberals win two bi-elections, one successful candidate is from Saudi Arabia and the other from China. As the year passes a split occurs in this party and the New Australia Party is formed.

Bill and I are enjoying a quiet drink after having tucked up our girls for the night. We turn on the television and the usual presenter is making an announcement about an important news item. Suddenly the screen changes to an outdoor broadcast and there is Mohamed Raman looking serious and handsome being interviewed outside his home.

The reporter thrusts a microphone into Raman's face and says rather abruptly, 'Can you tell us Mr. Raman what has led to this split?'

Raman moves back slightly, as if he finds the reporter's pushiness rather offensive, but then gives his memorable smile and proceeds to summarise the areas of disagreement between the Liberals and his New Australia Party.

He says his party wishes to see a continuation of limited immigration, not the total cessation as advocated by the Liberals. He also talks of how his party sees a need to introduce a programme of suitable education for all, replacing the wasteful and inefficient programmes currently in force.

One of his party's major points of difference is with regard to defence. He considers the massive spending on more planes, ships and army personnel, thought necessary by the Liberals, as wasteful and aggressive. His party would limit spending to defensive weaponry, and thus save an enormous amount of money that could be better spent on infrastructure, health and education services. He points out that in this way we would be showing a face of peace to the rest of the world.

While these policies are being outlined the reporter has been listening rather impatiently and as soon as Mohamed pauses he breaks in, 'And how many members are there in this New Australia Party Mr. Raman?'

'There are eighteen of us at present.'

'Is the split based on ethnicity?'

At this question Raman's smile vanishes and he answers coldly, 'Have you not been listening to what I have been saying? No, the split is based on the need to bring fairness and equity for all in this great land of ours. In answer to you rather rude implication we do not represent any specific ethnic group but have members from many different countries including native born Australians. This makes us the party that is truly representative of the multi-cultural land we have become. Now, good evening to you sir.'

With that he turns and walks up the path to his house leaving the reporter temporarily at a loss for words.

I turn to Bill on the couch and ask what he thought of what has virtually been Raman's policy speech.

Bill answers cautiously, 'I don't know what to think. I've never quite trusted him, and I would have thought it would be too soon for him to be rocking the boat like this. He's been in parliament for less than two years and he's already organising a new party.'

I've been an admirer of Mohamed Raman's since we met him before the election so I jump to his defence, pointing out that there have been plenty of other party splits in the past. I mention the Democrats and also how that long-standing and influential politician, Robert Menzies, had left Labor and started the Liberals sometime back in the middle of last century.

Bill answers, 'Yes he did but he'd been in politics for years. This guy hasn't the necessary experience to lead a party,'

I know Bill doesn't like Mohamed Raman for some reason so I simply say, 'I guess only time will tell,' and rise to get us another glass of wine.

2030 - 2034

Liberals and the New Australia Party form a coalition but it proves to be an uneasy alliance and an early election is called in 2030. Labor attempts to make a comeback under an aging Geoffrey Curtis, and field candidates in most electorates but they lack the fire and vitality of the representatives of the New Australia Party.

As usual Bill and I hold an election eve party, but by now our circle of friends has changed, and our guests are a less homogenous group than on previous occasions. Several of the teachers from our college are from Saudi Arabia, China and India and one of Bill's closest friends, Sam, is a refugee from the small island nation of Kiribati. He had been completing his master's degree in Australia when global warming destroyed his low-lying island home, and Australia had given refuge to all its inhabitants.

As I look around the room at the bright and varied costumes of the women and the varied skin colourings of those present, I think of how much we have changed as a nation in just one decade.

I have become an avid supporter of Mohamed Raman's New Australia Party and vote for him in this election. I don't know for whom Bill votes for because we haven't discussed our selections. Bill and I have rarely disagreed during our marriage, but in the weeks leading up to this election we've had several arguments about the policies of the three parties so made a pact to agree to disagree.

As I wander around the room talking to different groups of people I get the strong impression there is nothing like the cohesiveness of opinions there had been at previous election eve parties.

When Ruth says, 'Well at least Liberals plan on spending more money in an effort to solve the problem of overcrowding in the schools,' Gerry interrupts with, 'But they waste so much on keeping kids at school who couldn't care less about further education.'

Other parents in the group join in taking different sides about the effectiveness or otherwise of the current government.

I walk up to another group that includes Sam and Bill and Assad, as well as a couple of the new male teachers recently arrived from China. They are deep in conversation about climate change, and the degree to which Australia should be involved with helping other countries advance technically. There is obviously as much disagreement amongst this group of men as there is between the three major parties. I listen for a while, but then they begin to discuss some highly technical aspect of hot rock technology. I don't understand what they are talking about so drift off.

I join the group in the television room. Such a short while ago we'd had to crowd around to get to see what was on the screen, but now we have a screen that takes up one wall. Several people sprawl on the low lounges in comfort while they sip their drinks and listen to the commentary from the tally room.

I sit down next to Suzie, one of my friends from college, and ask, 'How's it going. Do they have enough votes in yet to make a call?'

Suzie's husband Bob replies, 'No. It's still very unclear what the outcome will be. The Curtis Government is getting barely any votes, the Liberals aren't polling well enough to win a majority and the New Australia Party is doing way better than any of the pundits thought they would.'

Suzie butts in, 'Actually Bob is refusing to recognise it, but the New Australia Party could achieve a majority. They're polling strongly in several of the marginal seats where they weren't expected to do all that well.'

Bob interjects, 'That's just wishful thinking on Suzie's part. They haven't got an ice cream's hope in Hell of winning a majority despite the millions that they put into their campaign.'

Obviously the differences of opinion that have been simmering in our household has also been taking place between these two.

The party continues until the small hours of the morning, by which time most of our guests are quite drunk, some have become argumentative and I am just plain tired. No one political party has enough votes to form a government. As everyone departs there is a mood of bewilderment rather than the celebratory atmosphere of previous years.

The outcome of the election is that no party has an outright majority and the Liberals and the New Australia Party once more form a coalition government. The leader of the Libs is prime minister and Mohamed Raman his deputy. Problems continue with this alliance because there are so many areas of disagreement, but progress is made in some sectors particularly in education. This is what most people think at the time.

Our girls are at high school now and we are very happy for them to be attending an all-girl school after being at a co-educational primary school. They are both clever and hard-working, and say it was much more peaceful being in classes without boys.

Segregation in all schools is being introduced throughout the country and several vocational colleges are being built. In time this will affect the matriculation colleges, but so far we have experienced little change at our college.

With regard to immigration, the Liberals call a halt to any further entries except in very exceptional circumstances. This is evidently a cause of great friction because Raman's party want a continuation of selective immigration. The Liberal's compromise, but insist that migrants should be able to demonstrate a high level of competency in the English language before being eligible for citizenship.

The two parties also reach agreement with regard to changing from compulsory voting; a practice that has set Australia apart from many other countries in the western world.

The greatest cause of contention between the two parties is in relation to defence, and on this they are diametrically opposed. The Liberals want to spend huge amounts on new weaponry and an increased armed force, while the New Australia Party push for defensive weapons and for a deployment of the members of the armed forces into employment within the country. Their differences in this area cause this coalition to become almost unworkable, but they limp on until the next election.

To me it seems that Raman's party is more forward thinking and would be better economic managers than their coalition partners. Their ideas with regard to defence seem much more logical and advantageous. By concentrating on defensive weaponry we would lessen the need to buy further expensive attack planes and ships, and many members of our existing armed forces could be employed in industrial and infrastructure projects.

Like me much of the voting population was beginning to feel that the more old-fashioned Liberal Party is holding back their more innovative coalition partners.

Once the election is called in 2034 the New Australia Party mount the most active and expensive campaign and stand members in every electorate. Many of their candidates are from other countries, but an equal number are Old Australians.

During the lead up to this election Bill and I have numerous heated discussions. I am a strong supporter of the New Australia Party, but Bill retains his suspicion of Mohamed Raman.

During one of these discussions Bill says, 'I'm never quite sure what he means when he talks about suitable education and employment. The fellow comes from an elitist background and has a different outlook from us.'

I answer, 'You're just being racist. Mohamed Raman is concerned for all, and has the vision and drive to pull our country together, and deal with the unemployment and financial problems that are a legacy of the previous governments.'

On another occasion Bill says rather sarcastically, 'Have you noted how few female candidates they have? You'd be lucky if there are ten standing in the whole country. I'm surprised you aren't concerned about that.'

To tell the truth I really hadn't paid much attention to this fact, but answer belligerently, 'There aren't many women standing in the other two parties either. It's always been like that in Australia.'

That year we don't host an election eve party and neither do any of our friends. In the lead up to this election discussions have been rampant and caused divisions between many friends and their spouses. Australians had always been fairly laconic about their political parties and leaders, but Raman's charismatic personality has sparked an interest previously lacking, and engendered strong emotion both positive and negative. He has polarized the country, and everyone seems to prefer to watch privately as the results unfold rather than in a social setting.

At the beginning of the evening Bill and I watch the television in different rooms. He has known how I would vote and that we are barracking for different parties. As a result of this difference of opinion we have resorted to the rather childish behaviour of watching separately as the results come in.

When it becomes apparent the New Australia Party has won a resounding victory Bill joins me, and we listen to Mohamed Raman's acceptance speech together.

It is a brilliant and positive speech. As a sort of peace offering Bill says, 'Well the fellow certainly sounds sincere. I just hope he lives up to everyone's expectations; if what we hear is what we get.'

Then he rather spoils his attempt at peacemaking by adding as though as an afterthought, 'Did you notice the way his wife stayed in the background and didn't join him on the podium? I don't think there'd be much freedom of choice in that household'

I am tired of the bickering that has been going on between us during the past weeks so let this remark go unanswered. I can't help feeling, however, a slight tremor of apprehension at the sight of that small, burka-clad figure standing silently in the background.

I still have a copy of Mohamed Raman's speech as it appeared in the newspaper the following day. The print is faded and the paper thin, but it is still readable. Today, as I make this copy, it is with a different understanding than I had back then.

There is a photo of Mohamed Raman standing on the podium with both his hands above his head in a victory wave. He looks sleek and handsome and is smiling widely. The complete text of his acceptance speech appears beneath this photograph. There are the usual words of thanks to his supporters, party members and family and general comments about the campaign. It then continued with the promises he made which so many of us believed in implicitly.

I will copy the final section in its entirety so that anyone who might read this in the future will perhaps understand why so many of us put such faith in him to lead us.

'Finally I want to say that I am honoured to be given the opportunity to represent this great country of ours as the leader of the New Australia Party.

The previous government, in which my members and I played an active role, has set our country on the road to economic stability. We have slowed the rate of immigration, and this will flow onto a drop in unemployment. We have also reversed the wasteful educational policies of the previous governments, and are in the process of implementing a policy of suitable education for all.

As your new leader I will make this country of ours a genuinely New Australia. Although I have my roots in another land I have been a citizen of Australia for over a decade. I have seen our country change from one in which the monarchy of Britain remained its titular head; a country that blindly followed the United States with regard to international affairs resulting in our participation in unjust wars. During the past decade we have grown, and we are now ready to take our place as one of the leading countries in the world. We have the technology, we have the wealth and now we need to organise some of our internal problems.

My aim is to create a land where all people live in harmony, and where each person is gainfully employed in work suited to their ability, education and training.

As your leader I will ensure that we never again follow another country into war, but remain neutral, while protecting our shores from any possible invasion with the latest technology.

Finally I want us to be a land where all are free to follow the religion of their choice. We are a richly diverse country made up of peoples from many different lands and cultures. Of course there are differences in our beliefs, but we should recognise that we all worship the same God and it matters not whether we worship Him in a mosque, a church, a temple or a synagogue.

We will not let religion be a divisive force in our country for we are all New Australians and we will make this country one of peace, progress and prosperity.'

As I reread those fine-sounding words I can still see why so many of us were blinded by the rhetoric, and why we gave such unquestioning support to this leader.

2034 - 2042

Throughout the next decade global warming continued and began creating enormous problems in parts of the world. The island country of Kiribati, where Bill's friend Sam and his family had lived, was inundated some years before as were several other low- lying island nation of the Pacific.

Compared with many other countries Australia had only been mildly affected by climate change before technological advances and the shortage of oil slowed the warming. Some coastal areas were inundated when the sea level rose more than a metre, but the only really heavily populated areas destroyed were the canal developments along the eastern seaboard. Drought became widespread, but the huge water reticulation works undertaken to divert excess water from the north solved this problem.

Other parts of the world did not fare as well. Besides the low-lying islands throughout the world disappearing under the sea, several coastal areas across the globe were inundated. In the Southern Hemisphere parts of Indonesia, Malaysia and Thailand were affected while in the north England and Japan lost considerable land to the rising tide. The people in Holland and Belgium were forced to flee to other countries, and Cuba, the Dominican Republic and most of Florida disappeared.

Besides the effects of the rising water level there was an increase in cyclones in tropical areas, and America experienced more frequent and ferocious hurricanes. Damaging earthquakes and mud slides occurred throughout the world with heavily populated parts of China and India being particularly affected. In Russia and Japan several nuclear power plants were destroyed by earthquakes resulting in the deaths of millions and in land being laid waste for hundreds of kilometres around these sites.

It seemed that our fragile earth was rapidly being destroyed by mankind's refusal to reverse our damaging ways.

Most of these events took place during the third and fourth decades of this century when we in Australia still had access to information about what was happening in the rest of the world. Now we only know what we are told, so I don't really have much of an idea about how other nations are faring.

In 2034 a World Summit was held with all countries participating in what was the last attempt to launch a combined effort to save the world. Because of the devastation that had occurred in Russia and Japan agreement was reached to shut down all nuclear power plants and decommission nuclear ships.

Agreements were made concerning the sharing of technology and caps on pollution levels were put in place, but there was little co-ordination. Countries became insular as they struggled to deal with various disasters caused by extreme weather events, and the prohibitive price of oil brought trade between countries almost to a standstill.

From the late thirties most Australians knew little of what was happening in the rest of the world. To be honest most of us were so involved in our own changing nation we didn't give it much thought.

From the time the New Australia Party comes to power many changes begin to occur, but the one that has the greatest impact on Bill and me and eventually on all females is in the area of education when total gender segregation in schools is introduced.

Because Bill and I are teaching at a matriculation college we are not initially affected by the changes brought about by this bill so don't think much about it or see it as a cause for concern. Oh! We were so short-sighted.

I suppose another thing that makes us complaisant is that our daughters are receiving a good education at their segregated, private high school. We don't realise they are the lucky ones, and the last generation of girls to experience this.

Within a few months of the New Australia Party coming to power the existing segregation is extended to all primary and high schools. No one sees this as a problem because for years it has been considered that both boys and girls benefited from being educated in different environments.

By now there are also numerous Muslim schools throughout Australia, which have always been segregated, as have many of the Catholic and other nondenominational private schools. The change in the state schools is seen as a natural flow-on when it occurs.

What is more insidious is the way in which the curriculum changes, theoretically so that both boys and girls will be given a so-called "suitable" education. The schools are funded accordingly. While the boys' schools are supplied with the latest technological equipment including a laptop for every pupil, the girls' schools are generously supplied with musical instruments, sewing machines and the materials for art and crafts. They also have state-of-the-art kitchens installed where even very young pupils are taught to cook.

These changes have been in place for several years before we teachers at the matriculation colleges begin to notice a difference in our enrolments. In 2036 there were an equal number of boys and girls in our courses, but four years later boys outnumber the girls three to one.

In 2038 Fiona graduates from university. There are still quite a lot of girls still receiving their degrees at the graduation ceremony but both Bill and I are surprised by the extent to which overseas students now outnumber the Australians. For decades overseas students had been welcomed by the universities throughout Australia as they paid high fees to gain a degree here compared with Australian students. I guess once the family reunion bill was passed many parents in other countries would also have seen this as a way of gaining the means of migrating from their countries where pollution and global warming were beginning to cause havoc.

Ruth and Gerry's daughter Phoebe is also graduating and we take the girls out to dinner after the ceremony.

It begins as a lovely evening with us all so proud of our daughters. The girls have seen a lot of each other during their student years and are close friends, but we parents had lost touch to a large extent and are pleased to catch up again.

We go to dinner at a very popular and expensive restaurant not far from the university. The place is packed with parents like us who are treating their sons and daughters to a celebratory meal. Many of the students still wear their caps and gowns over their clothes, but Fiona and Phoebe have removed theirs in order to show off their new dresses.

Fiona looks stunning. She has inherited my height and people say she looks like me, but I can't believe I ever looked as beautiful as she does tonight. Her long black sheath suits her to perfection, and over it she wears a floaty black shawl streaked with a swirly pattern in gold and red.

By this time Joe and Fiona are engaged, but he doesn't join us until after dinner. I think he realises that this is a special time for parents to share with their student son or daughter, the culmination of parental ambitions for their child.

After we finish eating, Joe and Phoebe's boyfriend join us for celebratory drinks. They then go over to a group of their friends at a nearby table before going somewhere to dance.

Once the young ones leave we parents take the opportunity to catch up with each other's lives.

Jerry owns and manages two of the most exclusive boutiques in the city and Fiona and I had gone to one of these to buy her graduation dress. We had both been surprised by both the limited range available and by how expensive the clothes were. I tell him of our visit to his shop and ask how his businesses are faring, now that trade between nations has become so expensive.

He shrugs nonchalantly but a frown appears on his handsome face. 'I'm still making a buck but it is becoming increasingly difficult to source suitable clothing. And of course everything going up in price because of high fuel costs. As far as I can see things are only going to get worse with regard to all our imports, not only clothing.'

We talk about certain shortages we have already noticed occurring and the increased price on all imported foodstuffs, then as inevitably happens when teachers get together the conversation turns to education and the changes that are happening.

Bill says, 'I'm beginning to see a difference in my maths classes. For a while there I had more girls than boys in all my classes, but now that has reversed again and I only have boys in the advanced maths class.'

Ruth says rather angrily, 'You're only seeing the beginning of the end as far as a decent education for girls is concerned.'

I am surprised at the anger in her voice because years ago she'd complained about overcrowding in schools and I'd thought she would have approved the changes the New Australia Party has put into practice.

I say, 'I'd have thought segregation would've made things better for primary school teachers. What's the problem?'

'The problem is we were misled by Mr. Raman and his master plan for a so- called "suitable" education for all. We now must teach girls the subjects deemed "suitable" by his government. Our girls are taught only very basic maths, we have great kitchens but no computers and our school libraries are pitiful collections. No one dares complain for fear of being sacked or worse.'

'How terrible. I had no idea this was happening,' I put my hand on Ruth's arm in sympathy.

She pushes it away with an angry, 'You don't know the half of it. No one does unless they're in the situation. Only a few weeks ago two of our younger staff members complained to the principal when the last of our computers were requisitioned. Apparently they were needed at one of the boys' schools. Well because of their complaint these young women were required to attend a week-long retraining course at the Educational Institute.'

'I've wondered what that was used for. What happened there?'

'None of us really knows. They won't talk about what went on, but since they've returned they are different. Do you remember that old movie, "The Stepford Wives?" I nod my head and Ruth continues. 'Well they're a bit like them, all sunny and cheerful and happily toeing the line.'

I gasp in horror and splutter something like, 'I had no idea.'

Ruth interjects crossly, 'You're the same as most people. Unless something affects them directly they just don't care.'

I feel suitably reprimanded and Gerry fills in the awkward moment by saying something soothing, but Ruth remains quiet for the remainder of the evening. I feel sorry for having upset my friend, and ashamed of myself for being so unaware of how grim things were for teachers in the girls' primary and high schools.

Shortly after graduation night the 2038 elections are held, and there are several protests held outside the polling booths as well as on the steps of Parliament House. The protesters are mainly women teaching at the girls' schools and mothers of daughters. At the time I wonder if Ruth is taking part in the rallies, and search for her face amongst the crowd of angry women when one is shown on the television news.

I think most people dismiss them as malcontents, but she has made both Bill and me more aware of what is going on. We begin to wonder about what more changes we can expect.

Once more the New Australia Party is elected with a huge majority. The other two parties are seen by most voters as hopelessly old-fashioned compared with this vibrant new party that is getting things organised. In four short years they have spent billions on renewable energy plants, munitions factories to produce the rockets that will protect our land and has reorganised the armed forces. Many of the older servicemen have been retired on generous pensions. The younger ones become members of the National Militia, and are employed in factories and other work sites overseeing the civilian workers or as special members of the police force. A select few are retrained to become members of the elite Internal Security Force.

If we feel concerns about some of the policies, as a nation we accept the changes. We feel our leader knows what is best for the country, and we follow him like lambs to the slaughter.

The 2042 election is a farce. By now the Liberals are failing to attract new candidates, and most of the older members have left for the corporate world or retired on large pensions. Geoffrey Curtis tries valiantly to rally his party, but he has the look of a worn-out, aging has-been. He tries to remind voters of how his party had pulled Australia out of the recession and set the stage for the rapid advances Australia subsequently experienced, but it is too long ago and people only remember the problems associated with his leadership.

In this election voting is no longer compulsory. The Bill to make it non-compulsory had been put to the parliament by the New Australia Party. Raman argued that the right to vote was a privilege and it was nonsense to make a privilege compulsory. This Bill was passed almost without comment from the population at large.

For years many Australians had complained about having to vote, and pointed to the fact that in most other Western countries the people had a choice. It had been seen by some as something we were forced to do, like paying taxes.

This change, however, ensures the success of Raman's Party. It would appear, when given a choice, most people will vote for potential winners, but few bother casting a vote if they think their preferred candidate has little chance of success.

The result is that only about sixty percent of the eligible population vote, and they are overwhelmingly supporters of the New Australia Party.

That election is the last held in Australia. From that time Mohamed Raman is undisputed leader of the country, and he has his National Militia and highly trained Internal Security Force to enforce his laws and commands.

2032 - 2042

I seem to have skipped the years from when Fiona and Jill were little girls till the time when they had become young women, so I must retrace my steps. They were important years, and times of change for young ones because of how life in Australia became so different.

During the girls' teenage years there is nowhere suitable for young girls to go for entertainment, so we change the big garage area into a rumpus room and build on a carport for our cars. From the time the girls are in their early teens this is their space, and here they hang out with their girlfriends and later with a mixed crowd of boys and girls

When I was young my girlfriends and I went to pubs or nightclubs, to drink and party, to listen to bands and meet boys. By the time Fiona and Jill are in their teens these places are unsuitable for any respectable girl to frequent. They are full of men, mainly men from the Middle Eastern countries with a smattering of Old Australians.

Middle Eastern girls and women don't go to places of entertainment except to the movies. When Bill and I go out to see a film we sometimes see them. Generally they are in a large group, and always accompanied by a male relative. Some of these groups wear colourful flowing dresses and matching headscarfs, but others wear black burkas that cover them completely except for their eyes.

Few Chinese or Indian men frequent the pubs for they are not to their liking. Many clubs open that cater specifically for these ethnic groups. These clubs are for both men and women and they provide a reminder of home where they can listen to familiar music while they drink and dance and meet potential partners from the same racial group. Although Australia has become a very multiracial country there are few marriages between the different racial groups.

Not many Island men go to the hotels or nightclubs, because they mainly entertain each other in their homes.

Bill and Sam have continued their friendship and he and his wife Lottie come to dinner parties at our place. Their two little boys are much younger than our girls, and our daughters play with the little ones and put them to sleep in the trundle beds they each have in their rooms. For the girls it is a bit like having a live doll to play with and fuss over, and they leave us all free to enjoy the evening.

When we go to parties at their place they always insist on us bringing the girls. Unlike us Old Australians, who normally hire a baby sitter to mind our children while we socialise, the Islanders take their children with them wherever they go.

Sometimes they hold a hangi. For these a fire is started early in the morning, and a whole pig or sheep placed in the coals to cook slowly for several hours. Later vegetables are added and by nightfall everything is ready. Adults and children then feast together under the stars. When the little ones tire they are tucked up in beds or on couches, or else drowse happily on their parents' laps. They are lovely, happy evenings.

Fiona is very popular and has numerous boyfriends from the time she is in her early teens, but she isn't serious about anyone until she meets Joe. I can see from the first time she brings him home that he is the one for her.

They met at a rally. It is typical of Fiona that she would meet the love of her life while in the middle of a protest.

She had always been feisty and was frequently in trouble at school for speaking out about any unjustness or unfairness in the classroom. Her teachers loved her for her intellect and energy, but I recall one of them saying to me, 'She has so much talent and intelligence, but she needs to control her passions.'

I remember laughing with Bill after I told him about this assessment of our daughter.

Once she goes to university she is in the thick of protests. She comes home from the protest rallies bright-eyed and rosy-cheeked and absolutely beautiful in her certainties.

Some of the rallies involve internal university politics, like gaining longer hours of access to the library or the need for improved housing for overseas students.

Others are about broader, societal concerns. When I see her heading off to a rally I remember my disappointment that none of my fellow students protested against the cruelty being meted out to refugees or the lies we were told about the boat people and their reasons for trying to come here. We were a smug, insular generation who took the good life we were living for granted and didn't care that much about what was happening in the rest of the world.

I recall the first protest rally in which Fiona was actively involved. At that time she would only have been about thirteen. The Liberal Party was in power in a coalition with the New Australia Party, and it looked as if the previously open migration policy would be stopped. She, along with many of her student friends, opposed any changes to the existing policy and protested against it.

I remember this one in particular because it led to arguments between Bill and Fiona. He felt there should be a moratorium on further immigration until our internal problems with unemployment were solved, while she felt it was inhumane to prevent people in need from having a better life in our country. I have never forgotten this, because it was unusual for there to be disagreements in our home.

The rally at which she meets Joe is about the need for Australia to share our technology with less developed countries. By this time we are world leaders in solar and wind technology, but we are only sharing our expertise with countries that can pay for it.

Fiona and Joe come into our house, arms entwined, with Fiona laughing up into his face.

She says, 'Mum, this is Joe Edgerton,' and I know from the way she says this that she is telling me, 'This is the one.'

From this time they are almost inseparable and Joe, who is living in digs, becomes part of our family. He frequently joins us for meals, and at weekends often helps Bill with chores around the house. Bill treats him like the son we never had.

Joe's parents farm a sheep property that has been in the family since early settlement, and they are as happy as we about the coming together of our two children.

We meet them at the engagement party they host at their farm, and Joe's mother Betty and I are soon good friends. Together we plan the reception and help each other choose our wedding outfits. She is one of those easy-going, countrywomen and fun to be with because she gets pleasure from the smallest things.

Joe's two younger sisters and Jill are to be the bridesmaids, and the girls become close as they plan their dresses and go together for fittings.

Shortly after Fiona begins working in the City Library she and Joe marry in the little country church where he had been christened. The reception is held on the wide verandah of his parents' beautiful, old homestead.

The young couple set up house in an apartment in a block of flats that overlooks the river. They live there happily until a couple of months before Joanna is born, at which time they move to a small house only a few streets away from our home.

Compared with this uncomplicated courtship and marriage, Jill and Ali have to contend with doubts and wariness from both his family and ours.

They meet when Ali comes to collect his niece who is in Jill's class. He is instantly besotted with our pretty, blue-eyed blonde daughter, and begins to pick up his niece regularly so that he can get a chance to talk to her teacher.

Jill is initially a bit wary of this dark, handsome man who gazes at her so intently and holds on a little too long when they shake hands in greeting. Because she attended a segregated high school and has only socialised with Old Australian boys at university she is unfamiliar with the ways of Arab men, and unaware of the restrictions in their culture surrounding courtship and friendship between the sexes.

The meetings at school are soon followed by the arrival, almost daily, of huge bouquets of flowers so that our home begins to look like a florist's shop.

Next Bill receives a very polite letter in which Ali requests permission to court his daughter. We have a quiet laugh about this, and decide to invite him to dinner. Of course Jill has discussed her flower-sending suitor with us, and told us she definitely finds him attractive so we all look forward to getting to know him better.

He arrives with flowers for Jill, chocolates for me and a bottle of very old port for Bill. During the meal he talks seriously about his family, his job with the Civil Service and the house he is planning to build. It is almost as if he is applying for a job and filling us in on his credentials. I find him very appealing, and from the look on Jill's face so too does she.

While Bill and I load the dishwasher and make coffee the young couple sit together on the couch, deep in conversation, and when it is time for our guest to leave Jill shows him to the door. She returns to the lounge room with a smile on her face and slightly smudged lipstick.

Their gentle courtship continues like that for several weeks, and then we receive an invitation to dinner with Ali's family. None of us is quite sure what to expect from the evening for Ali had told us his family is very traditional. Jill and I wear our most concealing clothes, long dresses with matching headscarves.

We had been told that a car would be sent to collect us, but are still a bit surprised when a black stretch limousine driven by a chauffeur pulls up outside. Ali comes to the door and is soon shepherding us into the car's luxurious interior. He is obviously nervous and keeps running his hands through his black curly hair, a mannerism of his that I had noted on other occasions when he has felt ill at ease.

The driver takes us over the bridge and along the eastern side of the river where there are a scattering of houses set on large blocks of land. We enter at a high wrought-iron gate, which opens as we approach, then drive up a wide tree-lined avenue before stopping in front of the house.

It is a huge stucco-rendered cream building with wide steps leading up to a tiled verandah. As we get out of the car I see Ali's entire family assembled there to greet us. The men stand in front and the women hover in the background.

We are introduced first to his father, a large heavily set man with black, curly hair, bushy eyebrows and a long, curved nose above full lips and a strong chin. Seeing him I can see how Ali will look when he is older.

The father introduces his two older sons then his wife and daughters-in-law.

Ali's mother is a little butterball of a woman with a sweet smile, and the girls are both darkly beautiful but seem very shy. They don't take my hand when I proffer it but nod and avert their eyes.

Ali has told us about his family, and how both of his two older brothers are in marriages that had been arranged by the families.

When he told us this he said, 'I have had disagreements with my parents because I would not follow this custom. I always felt there was a special one waiting for me to find and I was right.'

He looked at Jill with such love when he said this Bill and I lost many of our misgivings about those two.

After the introductions Ali's mother takes my arm saying, 'You probably need to freshen up. Come with me.'

As it has only been about twenty minutes since we left home I don't think I am all that travel worn, but we all troop into the house. We go up an ornate, curved stairway and into a powder room, which is as large and luxurious as any you would see in a five-star hotel. I renew my still fresh lipstick while the girls chat quietly to Jill, admiring her dress and hairdo. We then descend the stairs and are led into the dining room.

Ali's mother takes the seat at the bottom of the table and indicates that Jill and I are to sit either side of her. The two girls sit next to us and then we are joined by the men who sit at the other end of the table. This seems very strange to me, as it is so different from the seating arrangements I am used to at dinner parties. I look along the table to Bill who gives me a quizzical grin.

We are to learn later that normally the women eat in a separate room from the men, and this shared meal is a concession made for our visit.

The meal is sumptuous and two pretty Island girls serve us. While we eat the men talk about soccer and work while we women chat about clothes, shopping and cooking. At no time do the conversations meld.

As soon as we finish eating Ali's mother rises saying, 'We will leave the men to their cigars,' and leads us from the dining room into a small adjoining sitting room. I am beginning to feel like a bit player in a Victorian melodrama.

One of the Island girls serves us with tiny cups of coffee and little very sweet cakes, and then the daughters-in law take Jill off to show her their houses which are in the same grounds as the main house. As soon as the girls leave the room Ali's mother squeezes my hand and says, 'I am glad my Ali has found such a lovely girl for his wife. My husband wanted him to wed a girl from the family of one of our dearest friends but he refused. He has always been the most free-thinking of my sons, and he usually gets his way.'

As she says this she smiles fondly at the thought of her independent, youngest son and I get a strong impression Ali is her favourite.

I answer that I am sure they are well suited and certainly love each other very much.

She says, 'Ah, yes love,' with a dreamy look lighting up her round, pretty face. I wonder to myself if that look is for Ali's father or for some forbidden love of the past.

When the girls come back from the tour of inspection the men re-join us, and Bill says it is time we were heading home. He has a set look on his face that troubles me, but he is quite effusive when saying goodnight to the other men.

Once more we climb aboard the stretch limousine for the homeward trip. Bill and I are seated in the middle and I hear Jill asking, 'Were you expected to build in the compound the same as your brothers?'

Ali answers, 'My father wished me to, but I have always wanted a more separate life than my two brothers. I don't think you really grow up if you stay too tightly held by your parents.'

Listening in I am glad for Jill that he has this independent streak. I am sure she will be happier living apart from the extended family.

While we are undressing for bed I remember the way Bill looked when he and the other men re-joined us in the sitting room, and ask him how he had got on with Ali's father.

He scowls a bit and says, 'He asked some damned impertinent questions.'

I ask, 'What sort of questions?'

Bill answers, quite gruffly, 'You name it, and he asked it. Did Jill plan to work after marriage? What was our religion? Was she healthy? Did she want a lot of children? Had she had any serious boyfriends before Ali? He only just stopped short of asking me if she were a virgin. It was quite a cross examination I can tell you and he was starting to get my back up.'

To smooth him down I say that it's natural for him to be concerned because Jill and Ali have grown up with different life styles and in different cultures. I also remind him that we had been pretty wary about Ali until we got to know him.

Bill agrees and we lie in the dark talking about the evening, the opulent house and the partially segregated dinner party.

After Bill drifts off to sleep I smile to myself as I imagine the conversation that had taken place between Bill and Ali's father. I would have loved to hear Bill's answers to the "cross examination," particularly the questions concerning his daughter's love life.

Like many Australian fathers of his generation Bill was firmly convinced his daughters would remain pure and virginal until they married. In this he was totally wrong about Fiona who had experimented happily before finding Joe, but he may be right about Jill. She has always been more cautious and less daring than her older sister.

From the night of that dinner party planning for the wedding begins. We had never been practising Christians, so it doesn't bother us when Jill happily agrees to adopt her future husband's religion. It does mean, however, that all the organization of the wedding is completely taken out of our hands. It is done in the nicest possible way, but we can't help feeling sidelined even though we know we would be incapable of organising a Muslim wedding.

It is a big, colourful and expensive affair and after their honeymoon Jill and Ali move into the beautiful house he has built for them and in which they still live.

2042 - 2046

During these eventful years when both of our girls start work and then marry within a year of each other things are happening for Bill and me on the work front. We begin to notice changes, not only in mix of the sexes in our classes, but also differences in the abilities and achievement of the boys and girls under our tutelage.

The effects of educational changes in the primary and high schools are finally filtering through to the matriculation colleges by the early forties. For some time the boys had been out-numbering the girls in my English classes, but now generally boys are achieving much better results than the girls. My girls seem to lack a basic grounding in grammar, and most of them have a limited knowledge of literature. I begin to wonder what exactly they are being taught in the high schools, and if it is as limited as Ruth had said.

Along with all the other matriculation colleges our school is segregated from the end of 2043 and we female staff members are moved to a small stone building next door to the existing college. Female enrolments are now so small that I wouldn't have a full teaching load just teaching English, so I am allocated to teach History as well.

I am quite happy to do this as I studied both subjects at university, and my father had fostered in me both an interest in and a love of history while I was growing up. What surprises me when I first see the new History curriculum is the time span I am expected to cover. It seems to be too broad, as it takes in the earliest civilizations and progresses up until the end of the twentieth century. It is a potted history of most countries in the world.

I am concerned about how I can teach this course in a satisfactory way, but when I query the Principal about the enormous time frame to be covered she just pats my shoulder and says, 'Just do your best Marion. What our girls need is an overview of the past. They don't need to know the specifics.'

I am taken aback by her answer. She had previously been the head of the History Department at the college, and had a name for demanding academic rigour from both her staff and students. I leave her office feeling slightly bewildered by her remarks.

When I read the guidelines for the course I am to teach I am rather at a loss on how to proceed. I so wish I could go to my father to ask his advice on how best to cover such an extended period, but he died several years previously. I had, however, inherited all his books and lecture notes, and I spend the long summer holiday dredging through these to formulate a reasonably good course to teach my students in the coming year.

This is to be my first experience of having all girl classes and I rather look forward to it. I have never had many problems with discipline as by matriculation most of the young people are there to learn, but boys have inevitably caused any trouble that there was in the classroom.

From the first day I am surprised in my English class to find how little my girls know. They seem to have no knowledge that I can use as a frame of reference.

As with History I have been given the curriculum for English at the end of the school year and haven't had any problems with it. I think the choices are a little old-fashioned compared with what I have been teaching for the past twenty years, but can't quibble with the literary merit of texts to be studied. They include Shakespeare's

"The Taming of the Shrew" and Ibsen's "Hedda Gabler," poems by Rosemary Dobson and Les Murray and two novels, Charlotte Bronte's " Jane Eyre" and "One Hand Clapping" by our own Richard Flanagan. It seems a rather strange selection to me, but are all works I have taught in the past.

What upsets me as the year progresses is how difficult it is to stimulate any real interest amongst my students in the feelings and emotions expressed in the works they are studying. They hand in papers that are reasonably linguistically correct but which lack any real evidence of a deep understanding of the characters in the plays and novels. Few of my girls react positively to the poems, and this is strange for, in the past, poetry was a favourite amongst many of my female students.

My students are now like automatons who take in what I tell them they should feel and spew it out verbatim in their essays.

Out of about fifty students who I have in my two English classes only one has an original take on what she is studying, or even seems genuinely moved by any of the texts. Her name is Anne and one day she comes to me after class.

We have been studying the poems of Rosemary Dobson and she says she wants to talk about one particular poem. I hand her my book of poems and ask her which one she wants to discuss. She turn the pages until it opens at the one we had been discussing that afternoon which is "The Fever". She says in a quiet voice, almost a whisper, 'Oh, Mrs. Harper, I didn't think I would ever hear how I feel expressed as clearly as in that poem.'

Seeing that she is so moved by the poem I ask, 'Which part did you relate to so closely Anne?'

She begins to read,

'My mind like a white butterfly,

Moves from the curtain to the sheet,

From sheet to mirror, which returns

All it receives of sky'

Blushing she whispers, 'That's exactly how I feel.'

A bit surprised by the passion in her voice I ask, 'Why does it affect you so much?'

She answer with tears in her eyes, 'That's what I'm like. That's how I am. I feel there is so much more I need to know to make sense of what I'm being taught, but I am like the butterfly in the poem. I try so hard to understand properly what you're telling us, but I'm flying blind like that butterfly.'

I would like to be able to say that I offer to give her extra tutoring to fill in the gaps in her education, but I don't. I simply tell her she is doing very well and send her on her way.

She leaves school before the end of the year. When I hear that she has been forced into an arranged marriage to an old man shortly after leaving school I feel guilty for I know I let her down. I should have spent more time with her; should have stimulated her enquiring mind and helped to fill in the gaps in her education. I will always regret making light of her concerns when she came to me for help.

Teaching History is less frustrating than English because I don't expect an emotional response to the factual information I am providing. I try to make the lessons interesting, and take a leaf from my father's book by emphasising the lives of ordinary people during each period.

Because this is a trial curriculum observers often sit in on my lessons, but I don't mind this for I am pleased with my course and the girls' responses to it. By the end of the year I feel I have given them a broad, albeit surface knowledge of the history of the world. I am, therefore, surprised and very angry to be told this course isn't going to be offered the following year, and that I will be teaching Australian History instead.

Before the school year ends I make an appointment to see the Principal. I want to query the decision to scrap the history course I have taught because I feel that at least it has given my girls some knowledge of the past.

The Principal is a large middle-aged Scottish woman. Although I have known her for years we have never been close; her rather dour personality deterred other staff members from making overtures of friendship. Despite this we all recognised her as being academically brilliant and a good teacher.

When I enter her office she is seated at her desk, and she waves me to the chair opposite, a frown on her broad, plain face.

As soon as I am seated she says, 'I presume that you wish to discuss with me the course change in History Marion.'

I have brought along a copy of the course I had taught, as well as examples of some of the better essays written by my students during the year. I begin to make my case for continuing with it in the following year, but she waves her hands as if brushing aside an annoying insect.

'Before you begin let me say that I've been happy with your work this year, and would like to have seen you continue with it next year. This is not, however, my decision and there is nothing I can do about it. The Education Department is of the opinion that too many of our young people are ignorant about the true history of this great country of ours. It is felt that correcting this ignorance should take precedence over learning about the history of other lands and other times.'

I try to interject saying, 'But they are so ignorant about...'

I don't get any further before the Principal stands up and says, 'I'm afraid I can't discuss this further. You have a copy of the textbook to be followed next year. Read it and prepare your course based on that text, and I will assess it in the week before the commencement of the new semester'

Rather taken aback by her brusqueness I stand and gather together the papers I have brought to the meeting.

She comes from behind her desk and, placing a hand on my arm says, 'I'm sorry Marion. There's nothing I can do. You really would be wise to go along with this.'

I think I see tears in her eyes, but I'm not sure.

During the first two weeks of the summer vacation I spend many hours reading the history book on which I am to base my course for the following year. As a result I am in a constant state of agitation and anger, and I know I am making life unbearable for Bill.

When I become particularly upset about some section I read it to him. He tries to see some truth in the misinformation, but his attempts only annoy me. We argue almost constantly through these hot dry days, and our tempers flare as easily and quickly as the bushfires that are plaguing our country this summer.

The source of my anger is entitled, "The History of New Australia", but should be called, "The New History of Australia".

It begins quite factually with convict settlement, and the subsequent development of the nation up until the nineteen fifties. There is an over-emphasis on the evil characters of both the convicts and those who came as free settlers. It makes it appear that all of the original colonists were either convicts or the dregs of English, Scottish and Irish society.

There is also a complete section on the killings and mistreatment of the indigenous people in the early years of settlement, and the continued oppression and neglect of this group in our society. While I can accept that our record has not been great in relation to these original inhabitants, this book makes us look even worse than we have been.

With reservations I can accept this so-called history up until about nineteen forty or fifty, but I become gradually appalled by the way in which Australians and our way of life is depicted during the latter half of the twentieth century. I also have a very different opinion from the book's version of the past forty years.

When I become annoyed about this section of the book I insist on Bill sitting down while I read to him the section about the migration programme that commenced after the Second World War.

It explains that Australia needed to increase its population in order to remain strong enough to withstand the threat of a Communist take-over from neighbouring lands. A migration programme was initiated in which people from Great Britain and Europe were encouraged to settle in Australia. These migrants were given either free or very cheap passage on the understanding that they would work for two years as directed.

Bill says with a shrug, 'Well that's what happened. What's your problem with it?'

I wave the book angrily in front of his face and continue reading, 'Most of these migrants received extremely poor treatment in what was to be their adopted country. They were housed in sub-standard, communal compounds on their arrival. Usually they were forced to work in dangerous situations building dams and bridges or in the mining industry. They were based in isolated communities and lived in extremely primitive housing. When they visited the nearest towns or cities they were treated as social pariahs by the Old Australians.'

As I finish reading this part Bill says, 'Well I suppose it could be seen that way. I can remember your father saying what a difficult time many of the migrants experienced; that they were called Wogs and Krauts and Poms and were ostracised socially. And it's true that many of them did work in some very isolated and desolate places while they fulfilled their two year commitment.'

I interject, 'I know they did but after those first two years most of them made good lives for themselves and were assimilated into our society. This book implies that nearly all of them returned to the land of their birth, preferring to live in their own war-ravaged countries than stay here.'

At that point Bill really annoys me by saying, 'A lot of people did go back.'

I shout at him, 'Why do you always have to try and rationalize everything? I know some went back, but only a tiny percentage. According to this book nearly all of them left, and that we continued as an insular, underdeveloped country until we were "saved" by the injection of wealth and culture brought here by the Saudi Arabians, Chinese and Indians.'

Looking bewildered in the face of my anger Bill says, 'Look Marion, it's no good you reading bits of that book out to me and expecting me to make an informed comment. Give me the wretched thing so that I can read it in its entirety.'

Feeling totally infuriated with Bill rationalising what I know is a very biased and skewed view of Australia's more recent history I throw the book at him and stomp off for a walk in the park.

When I return about an hour later Bill is still where I left him, sitting on a bench in the garden and engrossed in the book.

'Well what do you think,' I demand.

'I'm only halfway through, but I can see why it's upsetting you so much. It's pretty scary stuff.'

'How can I possibly teach this? It's a totally skewed version of our history. It demeans Australia as a nation, exaggerates our shortcomings and completely ignores two centuries of social, cultural and scientific development. It even minimises our sporting achievements.'

Bill pats my arm and says gently, 'Let me finish it, and then we'll discuss it.'

That night we eat our dinner in silence, something unusual for us. After the meal Bill returns to reading the book, and I soak in a long, hot bath before going to bed.

Later that evening, while I am still lying awake mulling over how I can possibly teach this version of our history, Bill joins me in bed.

He takes me in his arms and says, 'My poor darling. I can see now why you've been so upset. Tomorrow we'll go through it together; see if anything can be done to salvage some of the truth from this material, and still get it accepted.'

For the next two weeks Bill works with me while we formulate the course. We follow the text with regard to early settlement and the treatment of the indigenous people, as it is close to the truth, but add a section on the developments that took place up until the 1950s. We soften the depiction of the treatment of migrants, and show the positive influences that have accrued from the inclusion in our society of the many who stayed.

Both of us have problems with the depiction of Australia as a country that had relied solely on the export of mineral and agricultural products to sustain itself economically. There is an element of truth in this but the book makes us look like a land of miners and farmers. To show other elements of Australian economic development we insert a section that includes the fact we produced our own cars, had at one time a vibrant textile industry and that we led the way in numerous medical and scientific break throughs. We don't know whether this section will be approved but hope that it will.

Our greatest problems occurs with the depiction of the years under the former governments. We know that in many ways both previous governments had been good for our country. Their policies had lessened the effects of the Global Financial Crisis, and their more open immigration policies had opened the way to Australia becoming one of the wealthiest and technically advanced countries in the world. They had created problems for themselves with the dramatic rise in the population, but by now Bill and I are seeing the even greater problems and unfairnesses that are occurring under the present government.

One hot January day we sat on the verandah with glasses of wine and the now hated book, and tried to complete what will be the last section of my course. The book depicts Australia now as a virtual Utopia, and Mohamed Raman as the saviour and founder of this brave new world.

Bill looks at me despairingly, 'What can we do with this? It's so full of half-truths and downright lies, but if we change it too much it won't get through.'

I have loved the way he has shared this problem with me and reach across to pat his hand.

'Perhaps if I mention what was good about the previous governments but then allude to the resultant problems, and then do the same with the Raman years, but emphasise the positives and merely suggest there may be some aspects of our society that are less than perfect.'

Bill answers ruefully, 'I wish you well with that bit my darling. Be very wary of how you present any faults.'

I send a copy of the finished course to the Principal as had been requested at the end of the previous year, and receive notification that it has been read and assessed. I am requested to attend a meeting at the college the following day.

When I arrive at the Principal's office at the designated time I am ushered in by the bursar, who also acts as the Principal's secretary. There is a new Principal sitting behind the desk.

I must show my surprise because I am instantly greeted with the words, 'Miss McGregor has left the staff. She has chosen to take voluntary retirement and I am her replacement. I am Jemma Robertson and I understand you are Marion Harper.'

Despite her English sounding name this lady is definitely of Middle Eastern origins. Going by her surname I think she must be married to an Old Australian and wonder what her husband is like, for she appears far too formidable and cold to have ever felt love for another human being.

She has jet-black hair drawn back from her face in a tight bun that emphasises her high cheekbones and dark eyes. She speaks the slow and almost mechanical way some people use when speaking in an unfamiliar language.

I step forward to shake her hand, but she ignores my proffered greeting and sits down behind the desk, waving me to take the seat opposite.

I can see she has the copy of my course open on her desk and without any preamble she says, 'This will not do Mrs. Harper. You have chosen to make alterations and additions that are not consistent with the text. What was your reason for making these changes?'

I had expected to have to give a good explanation for my changes, but had imagined I would be doing this with Miss McGregor. This woman slews me completely with her arrogant manner and cold stare, but I decide to bluff it out. Bill and I had worked long and hard to produce a course that is reasonably honest while still following most of the text.

I state with a confidence I'm not really feeling, 'I've made some changes where the text was lacking in detail or necessary information. I don't see why you find it unsatisfactory.'

She glowers at me and lowers her thick, dark eyebrows to such an extent her eyes almost disappear, 'You couldn't help but know that this butchered version of our country's history would not be approved. Having examined it closely, and having reviewed your employment record, I have come to the conclusion there are only two choices available for you. You can either enrol for a two-week course at the Educational Institute, where you will have a tutor to help you understand how to teach the required course, or you can take voluntary redundancy.'

I had heard rumours for years about the training received at the Institute, and although I have never known anyone who has been "retrained" I remember what Ruth had said about the two young teachers who behaved like "Stepford Wives' when they returned from there.

I know I have no choice but to take redundancy, so I answer with as much dignity as I can muster, 'If I can't teach the course I've prepared I no longer wish to continue as part of this so-called education system, so I will accept redundancy.'

'In that case I wish you to leave the premises immediately. You will receive a letter of termination and details regarding your financial entitlements in a few days.'

I turn on my heels, march out of the office and begin walking down the corridor to the small room I have shared with two other teachers. I am planning to clear out my desk and pack up the books that line the shelf in the small space I had occupied.

I haven't gone far before I hear my name called, and looking around see the so-called bursar, Elizabeth Page, hurrying after me.

Before our move to the separate college this woman had been a clerical assistant, but with the move she had been promoted to this position. All financial matters are still administered by male staff members at the main college so she is bursar in name only, but with her so-called promotion she became a little Hitler. She was forever complaining about not receiving timetables promptly, and inundating the staff with lists and memos. We teachers often laughed rather cruelly about her behind her back.

I wait for her to catch up to me.

She grasps my arm roughly and says, 'The Principal has instructed me to see that you leave immediately Mrs. Harper. Your belongings will be packed up and sent to you, but you must leave right away. I am to escort you off the premises.'

I catch a gleam of satisfaction in her watery-blue eyes and a barely concealed smirk on her thin lips. I see how she is enjoying this situation, and think she must have heard us laughing about her. She puts me in mind of a rather unpleasant girl from my school days who told tales to the teacher about minor wrongdoings of the other girls.

I brush her hand from my arm and answer coolly, 'It won't be necessary for you to escort me, but I would appreciate it if you would oversee the packing up of my possessions.' Then I load on the sarcasm, 'You should be able to manage that.'

I turn and walk away leaving her open-mouthed. I barely make it to my car before I burst into tears. I am not yet fifty-five, but have been banned from a job I loved because I want to teach at least a semblance of the truth.

By the time Bill arrives home from work I have drunk half a bottle of wine and worked myself into a fury. I tell him my news as soon as he is in the door. He instantly tries to take me in his arm, but I push him away saying, 'It's so unfair. All I've ever wanted to do was teach, and now that's become impossible. I don't even understand what's going on. Why are all girls being deliberately undereducated? What advantage can it be to the country to have half the population ignorant?'

Bill pours me another glass of wine and one for himself, and leads me to the couch.

With a huge sigh he says, 'I don't know quite why this is happening, but after reading that book I talked to a few men at the gym, asked the ones with sons about what their kids are being taught. Most of them are pretty vague, but it seems the boys at the state schools are only getting a very basic education too, and then are automatically streamed into the vocational colleges. Evidently for the past few years we've only been getting students from the wealthy private schools, where the parents keep an eye on what their children are being taught, and from the Muslim schools. What we're now seeing is the end result of Raman's policy of a "suitable" education for all. I'm just ashamed of myself that I didn't query what was going on sooner and why.'

'That's how I feel too. I've been the same as you, going with the flow. I just accepted it when I had less and less girls in my classes, and the small numbers in the girls' school after segregation.' I feel my eyes fill with tears and brush them away impatiently. 'I still can't understand why this has happened; why it was decided that girls didn't need an equal education and shouldn't expect to be employed'.

Bill sighed and then said, 'I'm sure the initial motivation was the high unemployment experienced after our population increased so rapidly. What better way to solve this problem than to make half the potential workforce unemployable? But it's gone further than that. Now it's not only girls missing out. Look at the boys who are in the state schools. They're getting a limited education and even the bright ones are streamed into vocational colleges instead of matriculation colleges'.

Bill's concern for the boys when they are so much better off than the girls makes me angry and I say sarcastically, 'Trust you to see the boys' side of things. At least they all get jobs.'

Bill answers calmly, 'Yes, but not necessarily work they would be capable of if they had been given the opportunity to be educated to the level of their ability. The way the education system works now isn't just about depriving girls of a decent education. It's all been a matter of the control and regimentation of the whole of our society'.

He angers me by his continuing sympathy for boys and his rational analysis of the situation when I am feeling anything but rational. I say crossly, 'Oh! I don't want to talk to you about this. You really can't see that it's so much worse for the girls.'

Sensing my anger Bill changes the subject by asking me if there is anything I can do about my forced redundancy.

I have already rung the Workplace Appeals Court, and I tell him they are going to send me some forms to fill in with my complaint.

'The man on the phone warned me there's a backlog. It could be several months before I get a hearing. Anyhow it will probably be a waste of time to even bother because the powers that be will say I refused to teach the required syllabus.'

I know Bill is feeling sympathetic for me but when he says, 'God, I'm glad I teach maths. At least they can't mess around with that,' I am furious at what I take to be his self-centredness.

I answer sarcastically, 'Well aren't you the lucky one,' before flouncing out of the room, and beginning to prepare dinner, loudly slamming around pots to show my irritation.

The forms arrive a couple of days later and I fill them in, making a case for my reinstatement as succinctly and rationally as I can.

With the loss of my job I also lose the companionship of my workmates, many of whom have been close friends.

Suzie rings me a few days after my dismissal. She wants to know how I am, and what actually happened to cause me to take redundancy. I invite her around for a drink and a chat.

At first she is evasive, saying she has some chores she has to do, but then she says, 'Damn it. Forget what I just said. I'll be there in ten minutes.'

As soon as I open the door to her she flings her arms around me and holds me close. Although we have been friends and workmates for years we have never been demonstrative with each other, so I am rather taken aback.

When she releases me I laugh, 'What brought that on?'

'I've been so worried about you. We were told you wouldn't teach the set syllabus and had refused counselling. That new Principal is one scary dude. She made it very clear we shouldn't phone or visit you, or our own jobs could be in jeopardy. Whatever did you do to upset the applecart?'

I explain to Suzie about the skewed version of history I had been expected to teach, and how Bill and I had prepared a course that was nearer to the truth.

Her reaction is very similar to Bill's in that she says, 'At least they haven't altered the music curriculum.'

I am so pleased to see her I don't react as angrily with her as I had with Bill.

I simply say, 'Well think yourself lucky. Now fill me in on what's going on while I get us a drink.'

We have a pleasant evening and I see Suzie a couple of times after that, but she seems nervous about being at my house, and I become such depressive company that after a few months her visits cease.

That year I am so down not even the birth of my dear little grandson can pull me out of my misery.

I am also quite unreasonably sharp with Bill who continues teaching maths at the boys' college. I know I'm often unfair towards him, but I am jealous that he can still have his career while mine has been terminated so abruptly. In a way it reminds me of what my grandmother told me about how she'd had to leave work. I feel that at last I understand exactly what she experienced, and feel much delayed sympathy for her.

I, however, don't have the comfort or responsibilities associated with the bearing and rearing of children the way she did. My daughters are grown women who are making separate lives for themselves. Now my work has been taken away from me I feel discarded and useless, and Bill bears the brunt of my feelings of frustration and anger.

Because we both taught we had always spent much of the time when we were together discussing our work and our students.

Now if Bill mentions a problem he is having at the college, or wants to tell me about some highlight of his day I stop him with the surly rejoinder, 'Well at least you're allowed to work,' or 'Aren't you the lucky one to have a job.'

Sometimes I don't even wait for him to mention his day, but greet him with some snide remark about 'consorting with the enemy.'

If he tries to point out that someone has to teach the upcoming generation I jeer and say, 'You're condoning what's going on by being willing to teach to a group of privileged, spoilt brats.'

I know I am being completely unreasonable and behaving like a total bitch, but I can't stop myself. I'm feeling so miserable I want him to feel as badly as I do.

Sometimes I am sorry for being such a grouch, make a special effort to tidy the house and myself, and cook him a really good dinner. The problem is I'm not happy being the little stay-at-home housewife, and when Bill compliments me on the meal I answer snakily, 'Yes, it must be nice for you to have me as a servant.'

Of course this ruins everything and Bill excuses himself after our silent meal, and goes off to his study for the remainder of the evening. I know I was being unfair towards him, but somehow I can't stop myself.

When I'm not just thinking about my own life, I sometimes wonder about the marriages of other women who have been made redundant or been retrenched to make way for the many men needing employment.

Affirmative action that favours men has been introduced in all work places. Now within the workforce there is a definite preference given to males because they are considered the primary breadwinners, and many married women have lost their jobs. I imagine there must be lots of women as unhappy as I, but I suppose there are some who have settled into the routines of just being housewives and financially dependent on their husbands.

I wonder how this has affected their relationships. Have some of the men become bullies and tyrants once their wives are no longer their equals as wage earners, and have the wives become more submissive because of their financial dependence?

I also wonder about the sort of lives and relationships young girls can expect to have in this society. I know many of the girls who I had taught at college hoped to become teachers at the girls' schools, nurses or carers at the few remaining Childcare Centres, but what happens to the ones who only complete year ten at the now segregated schools? The changes to their education means they are no longer equipped to do office work, most of the retail outlets are staffed by men, and the more menial tasks such as cleaners or kitchen hands are performed by Island boys. Their only choices must be to stay at home and help their mothers, or to marry young and start families of their own.

I think of what my grandmother said about the girls of her generation who had gone happily into marriages to escape their dead-end jobs. It seems that Australian women's lives have regressed by nearly a century. Or should say have been forced to regress.

In my initial misery I become very isolated, but later attempt to seek out other women in my position. Initially I decide to try to contact other history teachers who have also been made redundant. I am sure there must be others throughout the state who have baulked at teaching that rubbish. If I can find others in the same situation I think we could organise a protest of some sort.

I ring the Education Department and ask if they can give me a list of female teachers who have ceased work this year. I make up some story about wanting to set up a social network for retired teachers. I am told very abruptly that this information is not available.

As the months drag by I frequently spend whole days going over and over in my mind how I could have handled the situation differently. I wonder if perhaps I should have prepared a course that was closer to the text, but then I read again that so-called history book and feel angry once more at the way it skewed what really happened.

I begin to read obsessively every book from my father's collection that deals with aspects of Australia's history, and borrow any books I can find in the library about Australian politicians, scientists, doctors, artists, writers and musicians. These only reinforce my feelings of anger about the way in which I have been treated for wanting to teach the truth. It is almost as if I am punishing myself.

During this time I also become an avid television watcher.

From the time of its introduction into the country in the mid nineteen-fifties Australia was a nation of T. V. addicts. Babies watched the Tele-Tubbies and similar programmes with flashing images and nonsense words from the time they could be propped up in their carrycots. The Wiggles or cartoons entertained children while they ate their breakfasts, and adults flicked on the television switch as soon as they entered their homes after work.

I join the mob and I too become an addict.

All media outlets are now state owned and run. The change to state controlled media was made easy by the fact that for years two wealthy families owned most of the newspapers and radio and television stations. One of these family companies had been bought out by a consortium of wealthy Arabs back in 2030 and the other by a group of Chinese businessmen about a decade later.

The changeover to a totally state run media seemed to happen almost overnight, but undoubtedly involved secret deals and machinations about which the general public was unaware.

Once this change had taken place the number of available channels was reduced to three, one providing entertainment and educational programmes for children and the other two aimed at the adult market.

At the same time information available from the Internet was heavily censored. Initially this censorship was aimed at removing access to pornography, but it was rapidly extended to include any information deemed to be damaging to society.

Some people complained about the limited access to information, but the more vocal complainants disappeared. Rumours abounded about what happened to people who criticised government policy and most of us meekly accepted this further limitation on our freedom of choice.

When I tire of my obsessive reading I watch everything that is available on the television.

I mindlessly watch cooking and gardening programmes, "soaps" and celebrity interviews, but there are two programmes I never miss, and I analyse them as I watch.

The first is on once a week, late in the afternoon and is called "Our Country". For me this becomes compulsive viewing.

I sense there is a strong element of propaganda, aimed at reassuring the doubters in our society that all is well in this great country of ours, but in my vulnerable state I need reassurance. Although these programmes generally only add to my confusion I watch them avidly trying to sift fact from fiction.

The programmes deal with a different group of people in our society each week. One is about the Indigenous Australians and it shows the men, all now gainfully employed, working on the large kangaroo reserves that have replaced most of the cattle spreads. The scenery is magnificent. Across the vast flat plains thousands of kangaroos graze on native grasses watched over by the people who have lived alongside them for centuries. When it is time to kill some of the animals the men do it in the traditional ways with spears and killing boomerangs. The carcasses are then packed into refrigerated vans and taken to the nearest depot to be despatched by electric trains to the cities.

A voice-over tells of how lands had been destroyed and turned into desert by hard-hoofed cattle brought here by the unthinking early Australians. Now with only the soft-footed native animals roaming the land it is regenerating, and the Indigenous men who farm these creatures have rediscovered their sense of worth. They are once again following the path of their ancestors. I am nearly in tears as I watch these men, looking so free and happy, and remember how previously so many of the Indigenous Australians were seen before by white society as derelict drunks, living in shanty towns in desert country or sleeping in parks or riverbanks on the edges of the cities.

The women and children are now well housed on reservations, and schools have been built on each reservation to ensure that every Indigenous child receives a "suitable" education.

It seems to be a wonderful solution to the problems that living on the fringes of white man society has given these people, but I can't help wondering about the separation of families. Couldn't this be seen as another "stolen generation," but one in which the men are taken from their families instead of the children? How often do the men get the chance to return to their families, to play with their children and make love to their wives? Something else that concerns me is what will happen to the bright boy or girl who has the brains and ambition to want to be educated past ninth grade when this is deemed the suitable level of education for these children? Under this scheme there will be no Aboriginal child who becomes a teacher or lawyer or scientist in this future Australia. Despite the poor record of our treatment of these original inhabitants there had been quite a few who achieved success in the professions and the arts. I can't see that happening under the present regime.

Another programme is about the huge industrial growth we have experienced under the Raman Government. It features a munitions factory where defensive weaponry is being made and another where electric cars are being produced. The workers look like busy insects as they labour in their dark blue overalls overseen by leather-clad members of the Militia.

It looks a little too regimented to me, but all the men who are interviewed express their satisfaction. They talk about the high pay and terrific amenities, but something about this programme makes me uneasy.

Even after I have turned off the television this feeling continues and I try to think why I found it upsetting. While I'm pondering on this I remember the conversation Bill and I had after I was made redundant and what he had said about the boys in the public schools. Suddenly I realised the relevance of what he had been trying to tell me. My only worry had been the effect that the policy of a "suitable" education for all was having on girls. Bill's concern was that it was also having a fairly disastrous effect on all the public school boys who were being streamed into trades. Even the brightest amongst them would end up working in factories like the ones I have seen today because Australia has had to become a manufacturing country now we can no longer rely on buying what we need from other countries. Raman and his party are certainly taking the long view and although I hate what he and his party are doing to Australia I think I'm finally beginning to understand at least part of their motivation.

One programme deals with the new educational system, showing children learning happily in segregated primary and high school classes. There is a large section dealing with the vocational colleges, and the benefits of this form of schooling.

Once again, watching this programme, I feel for the really bright children who should be given the opportunity to continue with an academic education. Under the current system if they are girls or boys from working-class families they have no opportunity to matriculate or continue their education at a university. As a result of the policy of "suitable" education, the professions are closed to all except those children whose parents can afford to send them to expensive private schools and the boys attending Muslim schools.

Watching this I finally begin to see how so many of us in the teaching profession were duped and I feel ashamed that we let it happen. We were all so stupid.

Another episode is filmed at two of the Women's Retreats. This is the first time I've heard about these places, but evidently they have been set up around the country to cater for women who have been widowed, or those who no longer have a male family member to look after them.

One is built in an idyllic spot near a beautiful tropical beach and the other in a glorious temperate rain forest. All the women who are interviewed rave about how wonderfully well they are looked after, and how great it is to have the companionship of women of a similar age to themselves.

I try to imagine what it would be like to live with a bunch of women. I don't think it would suit me but then I also can't imagine a life without Bill. Although I am being unpleasant to him much of the time I really love him very much. After watching this programme I determine to try and be nicer to him.

The other programme I watch avidly is our leader's weekly speech. It is shown on both adult channels simultaneously, thus ensuring that most of the population listen. It is not compulsory viewing, but I feel irresistibly drawn to view it If Bill sees me watching it he says, 'I don't know why you torture yourself with that propagandist crap.' Despite his negative comments I continue to tune in.

Watching Raman on these weekly programmes I am reminded of my father telling me about Hitler; of how he could hold a crowd of thousands spellbound by his speeches. With my father I once watched an old film of one of the many rallies held in Nazi Germany, and I had seen how Hitler hypnotised the people with repetitions and slogans.

When I'd watched that scratched, old film I had wondered how this funny-looking little man could have such a sway on so many people. My father explained that the German people were still smarting from their defeat in the First World War, and that he rebuilt their feelings of worth and superiority by using the Jews and gypsies as scapegoats. By diminishing these people he made even the lowliest and poorest Germans feel superior.

When I first started watching Raman's speeches I had hoped they would give me a clearer, larger picture of what is happening to our society under his rule, but they only result in an increased feeling of being manipulated and confused with regard to his master plan.

I can see similarities between Hitler and Raman, although our tall, handsome leader bears little physical resemblance to the strutting, ugly man who had ruled Germany. The characteristics they share are more subtle than mere physical looks, but there are similar cadences in the voices and the same gleam of fanaticism in their eyes. Like Hitler, Raman is enforcing change on an existing society and replacing it with one that is new, although Raman appears intent on building one that is more complex and multi-layered than that of Nazi Germany.

Raman has aged little since the first time I saw him when he came to talk to our staff about his views on education and set all our female hearts aflutter. He is a little heavier, but his hair is still darkest black and his eyes as piercing.

On the surface he appears the most benign of despots.

His basic message is that Australia has entered a new age. Under his leadership we have left behind the old unprogressively insular ways of the past, and have now become a wealthy, technologically advanced, safe country with full employment for all men.

With regard to women, his message is that women can now enjoy the lives for which they were intended instead of having to be part of the hurly burly of the workplace. Now they have the freedom to stay at home and rear their children instead of having to leave their babies and toddlers in soulless childcare centres cared for by strangers. Even though I know how the rights of women have been eroded and opportunities curtailed, he makes a convincing argument that now women have the chance to live in ways that suit their inherent natures and skills. Mind you it isn't convincing to me but I can see how some women might view their more relaxed, albeit limited life style, as an improvement.

From watching these programmes I slowly understand how Raman is using one of the major brainwashing techniques of breaking down the victim's beliefs and feelings of self-worth. I slowly come to see how he is taking away the pride Old Australians had felt about their country, and women had felt about being considered equal to men in the workplace, and replacing these feelings of pride and self-worth with a sense of shame.

Seeing Raman in action I recognise how he is using the basic brainwashing techniques used in Nazi Germany by Hitler, where the victims had all feelings of self-worth stripped away, and were thus made amenable to whatever treatment was meted out to them.

Raman's oft repeated criticisms of Australia's past is aimed at destroying the pride that many older Australians felt about their land, and his mantra of "suitable education and employment" conceals his sexist and elitist plans that have been so divisive.

From my experience with the Education Department, I now know this sort of propaganda won't be necessary with the younger generation because of the history they are being taught. They won't grow up feeling pride in their country's past, but shame. The lives they now live under the present government will look good by comparison with what they are being taught has gone before.

Most of them won't remember the time when we lived in a free and democratic society; a time when we had a sense of pride in our small nation that, for its size, had achieved much in the fields of science, medicine and especially in sport. While it is true we had not always dealt fairly with immigrants from other lands, and had failed the original owners of this land totally we had achieved much. This is now being completely negated.

This new generation will only know what they are told. They will accept that they live in a just society, run by a seemingly benign dictator who has made dramatic improvements to what had been a slightly backward and dysfunctional country.

We have become a stratified society run by Middle Eastern, Chinese and Indian men plus a few wealthy Old Australians. The education received by boys is dependent on their religious and ethnic background, or on the wealth of their parents, as is their eventual employment. The rights of all women to a decent education and thus to equal employment opportunities has been totally eroded. Women have become the Jews of Australia.

With these thoughts and feelings welling up inside me I watch our leader in silent and helpless rage, but the following week I tune in again to see him. It's no wonder Bill get angry with me for watching these weekly speeches but I continue to do so for they feed my rage.

Throughout this time I sleep very badly and drink far too much. Bill insists I see a doctor and I return with tablets to cheer me up and others to help me sleep. I take the tablets and continue to drink, although it warns against this on the packets. Sometimes I am still wandering around, drugged and dazed and in my dressing gown when Bill returns from work. I am slowly killing myself for I feel like a useless pawn who has been thrown on the scrap heap.

Towards the end of the year I receive a letter from the Workplace Appeals Court giving me an appointment date and time. It states that if I will be attending I must confirm it in writing within a week or the appointment will be automatically cancelled.

By this time I am feeling so depressed and beaten I can no longer imagine standing up for myself, or for my right to work. I throw the letter in a bin and open another bottle of wine.

I try to pull myself together when the girls come to visit with their babies, but they are still aware of my depression. I think they tell their father that perhaps a move to a new house would help me.

After two years of watching me mooch miserably around the house Bill is willing to try anything. He and I had often talked about moving to something smaller after the girls both married, but we hadn't got around to doing anything about it.

Now he suggests that we start looking, and the house hunting begins to help me get over my depressive and obsessive behaviour.

After much searching Bill and I found this cottage where I still live. I loved it on sight, and said, 'They'll have to take me away from here in a box.'

Who knows how I will leave here now.

Although the cottage had been built in the 1970s it is in good condition, for it had been well cared for and upgraded through the years. There are solar panels on the roof that supply all the power needs of the house, and a large rainwater tank. The previous owners had been into self-sufficiency, and the large back yard is organised on permaculture lines with herbs growing near the back door, a grassed area with outdoor furniture on it, then vegetable patches on either side of a path that leads to a mini orchard at the back of the block.

The front of the block is steep, but there are two beautiful liquidambars either side of the drive and camellia trees and rhododendrons across the front and up the side. Although the framework of the garden is already in place there is still plenty of scope for me to make it my own.

Inside there is a cosy lounge room with a wood-burning fire, a spacious kitchen with the dining room at one end and three bedrooms. The large master bedroom has picture windows facing towards the city and the river, and then there is a good-sized bedroom next to that and a smaller room with a view towards the mountain. We decide straight away this room will be our library, and it becomes one of our favourite spots in the house. There is also a large bathroom with a spa bath, something Bill and I had never had but thought we would like.

Bill likes the house, but for me it is more than just an instant liking. It seems to wrap itself around me, and I know that here I will find the serenity so lacking from my life and mind during the past two years.

It is winter when we move in, and I immediately plant the front with a mass of bulbs that will flower in the spring and hardy annuals for a summer show. Out the back I dig over and fertilize the vegetable beds, and plant out lettuces, beans, peas and spring onions. I leave space for later plantings of carrots, zucchinis, tomatoes and corn. I am still grubbing around outside in filthy overalls when Bill comes home from work.

He picks me up, kisses my dirty face and says, 'Looks like I've got my girl back.' For the first time in two years I return his kiss with real warmth and love.

During that first year on the mountain my daughters also get their mother back. I finally feel like a fully functioning person again, instead of the wine-soaked depressive I had become after being forced to give up my job.

I also begin learning what a joy it is to be a grandmother. Bill installs a slide and swing on the grassed area out the back of the cottage, and in summer we buy a little paddle pool. Fiona and Jill bring the children to visit a couple of times a week, and we sit in the sun contentedly watching four year old Joanna organising her cousin Sara, who is a year younger, and her brother Thomas in all manner of games.

While the children play my daughters and I chat away happily about the books we are reading, new restaurants we've been to and of changes I am planning to make to the house and gardens. We also discuss more serious matters; talk about the effects that global warming is having throughout the world, the limited education girls are now receiving and of our fears for the future.

On a personal level Fiona talks proudly of the work Joe is doing, and of how much she misses him when he is away. Jill rarely speaks of her life with Ali, and only seems to have a vague idea about his work in the Department of Finance.

The house he'd built for them is absolutely beautiful, and he employs a housekeeper and gardener/chauffer to make life easy for Jill. She no longer drives herself, but a car is always available for her to be driven wherever she wants to go.

Fiona and I sometimes think she is losing too much of her independence because of Ali's paternalistic attitude towards her, but he appears to love her very much and she seems happy. Once she says how glad she is that he had insisted on living away from the family compound, as she wouldn't have wanted the semi-cloistered life his mother and sisters-in-law take for granted. I suppose compared with their lives hers is one of relative freedom.

During this first summer in my new house Jill is pregnant with her second child, and wears loose floating gowns with a matching headscarf, which she says is to protect her hair and fair skin from the sun, but that we know she pulls across the lower part of her face when she is in public.

At times Fiona and I tease her about the headscarf and say she's emulating her Muslim sisters-in-law. One day Fiona teases, 'Soon Ali will have you in a burka like the rest of the good Muslim wives.'

Jill just smiles and says Ali likes the way she dresses now, and blushes at our chiacking. Then we feel mean.

Fiona still wears shorts and tee shirts when she is in the back yard, but she pulls on a long skirt and covering blouse before she drives home. It has begun to be considered unseemly for women to be too uncovered when in public places.

Most of us have accepted this change because it happened gradually. I suppose in a way a lot of us have been affected by seeing so many Muslim women looking graceful and feminine in their long, flowing gowns with matching headscarves and Indian women in their beautiful silk saris. The contrast between them, and us in our jeans and pant suits is so marked these other women begin to make many of us feel less attractive and somewhat masculine. Tahani had had that effect on us women in the Mother's Group many years before.

Throughout history styles have changed constantly, and there has always been a strong element of manipulation with regard to what is fashionable so we seem to adopt the changes naturally. At first these changes in our clothing are gradual, a move towards softer, more feminine styles and ones that most of us embrace.

The next change is far less gradual, for by this first summer in my new home clothes have become very expensive. Perhaps our teasing of Jill is motivated in part by jealousy for she can well afford the costly gowns Ali likes her to wear whereas Fiona and I can now only buy the most basic items of clothing.

In retrospect it seems strange to me how quickly Australian women made the change from being able to wear virtually whatever they wished, to the generally drab and poorly made garments of today. The big change came suddenly when trade between countries became so limited because of transportation costs. Suddenly the cheap and varied clothes imported from China and other countries where wages were low were no longer available. We were forced to wear what clothes we already possessed until they virtually fell apart and then had to make do with a limited range of fabrics from which to make our own clothes. Any notion of being fashionable disappeared.

Australian clothing factories had ceased to exist in the previous century as they had been unable to compete with the cheaper labour costs in other countries. Now new ones needed to be built and by the forties Australian factories were producing woollen, cotton and hemp fabrics in a small colour range. The manufacture of clothing was mainly limited to that required by men and boys so the factories produced black and navy suits and uniforms, khaki and navy overalls and casual pants and white shirts. One factory produced blue shifts for women employed by the government and here white cotton pants and bras were also made. Apart from underwear women were now expected to make their own clothes.

For the women of my daughters' and my generations this was tremendously difficult for we had never learnt to knit or sew. Living through the decades when cheap and varied clothing was so readily available these had seemed unnecessary skills, but now they are vital. The current generation of school girls were being taught to sew and knit. In many households they took over the responsibility of teaching their mothers and grandmothers how to knit, draft a pattern, use a sewing machine and hand stitch a hem. It was ironic but in a peculiar way this made the education these girls were receiving seem of value. I had pitied them because they lacked the education and knowledge to participate in the workforce but now the skills they have acquired are valuable. Was forcing us all to relearn the so-called womanly crafts of sewing and knitting a way of showing us that these girls were receiving a suitable education and of reinforcing our place and function in society? I think it was but then I have become an old cynic.

The only available fabrics were white cotton or hemp or brown wool, and most of us stuck to fairly basic designs for we lacked the skills to attempt anything very elaborate. We made cotton and hemp shifts and kaftans and full skirts and simple blouses for summer and long brown woollen skirts topped with hand-knitted jumpers for winter. Lacking the necessary skills to make coats or jackets we settled for simple cloaks to keep us warm when out of doors. Some of the more adventurous used natural dyes on the white cotton fabric to add a bit of colour to their wardrobes but not many bothered. At one time the government promised that factories to produce women's clothing would be built once the production of essential commodities was in train but this never happened and we had no voice to demand that it should. Obediently we settled for our homemade garments of summer whites and winter browns and lost all sense of clothing as adornment or a fashion statement.

The exceptions were the Madams who all opted for purple as their signifying colour. I believe they used blackberries and blueberries for the dye. You see them on the streets in their purple garments for these ghastly women seem determinedly proud of their so-called profession and are treated with guarded respect by those in authority.

It is rumoured that their girls, who are referred to as Floozies, spend idle hours experimenting with natural dyes in order to have brightly coloured clothes that appeal to the punters. I don't know whether this is the case or just a tale put around to make it appear that those poor girls are more contented with their lot in life than they could possibly be. There may be an element of truth in this though, for on the rare occasions that Floozies are to be seen on the streets they are dressed in cloaks that are a sort of faded red.

2048 - 2050

Fiona returns to work in 2048. She and Joe have been married for about seven years, but he is often away because of his work and she feels the need of adult company. I understand totally how she feel because this was how I felt when my girls were little. I offer to mind Joanna and Thomas because by now most of the childcare centres have closed as there are fewer mothers in the workforce. The few centres that remain open are too expensive for all but the wealthiest of families.

This arrangement works out well for me. Having these dear little people to care for gives me back a sense of purpose I had lost when I was made redundant at work.

Initially things are much the same at the library as when Fiona had gone on extended maternity leave, but a year after she has been back at work the government decrees that segregation of the sexes should be extended to all public institutions including libraries.

During the next few months following this announcement changes begin taking place, and Fiona tells me about them when she calls in to collect Joanna and Thomas. The permanent staff members continue with their routine tasks, but a supplementary task force is responsible for the reorganisation.

At first these people spend some time assessing the collection, and then the library is closed for a week and the permanents are given special leave.

When they return the reorganisation is complete, and a barrier has been erected. The collection has been separated and so too have the staff members, with employees responsible for providing service in the area of their gender.

I know Fiona is concerned about the changes that have occurred, and she often tells me about the limited range of material now available for women. She can't understand why she and her fellow female librarians receive so few complaints from the public. It bothers her how accepting women have become.

A few months after the separation has been completed Fiona comes in as usual after work.

On this particular day she is extremely agitated, and her lovely face looks tense and unhappy. The children run to her for their hugs, but she holds Joanna and Thomas only briefly before sending them back to play with the blocks that are strewn around the lounge room floor.

As soon as they are out of earshot she flings herself into a chair and moans, 'Oh Mum, you won't believe what's going on in the library. The special task force has returned, and they are weeding out more than half the collection.'

I answer in what I hope is a soothing voice, 'Are you sure you're not exaggerating darling? After all, as you well know, every library collection needs weeding.'

She jumps up from the chair and begins pacing the room. Her whole body is taut as she paces back and forth as though trying to outmanoeuvre the frustrations and aggravations of her day. I feel frightened for her, for I know her anger is as pointless and self-destructive as mine had been when I was sacked. I want to hold her in my arms and comfort her, smooth away her tensions, but when I move to touch her she waves me away and flashes her eyes.

She reminds me of how as a little girl she didn't want hugs and kisses if she were hurt. She would come inside with a gashed knee or with a splinter embedded in a finger and stand stiffly while I removed the splinter or applied a band aid. As soon as I finished she would be back outside again.

Jill had been so different. She would cry mournfully over any little hurt, and curl up on my knee for comfort, enjoying the extra cosseting.

It's funny how you can see the way your children will be as adults when they are quite tiny.

I am pulled back from my reminiscing by Fiona almost shouting, 'But Mum it's more than just a normal weeding process of getting rid of books that are not being read or are in bad condition. They are withdrawing any books that show women as intelligent or humorous or real. Granddad used to tell us about how the Mongols destroyed the great library in Baghdad way back in the middle of the thirteenth century, and how the Muslim culture and knowledge of centuries was lost. To me what is happening is similar, but this is so selective and aimed at keeping women ill-informed and ignorant of the achievements of our sex. It will mean girls and women won't have access to decent literature, and won't be able to read about women who've done so much in all fields, science, medicine, sport and in all of the arts.'

I hate seeing her so upset and when she finally stops this tirade I try to calm her by saying, 'Aren't you taking this a bit far?'

She silences me with a wave of her hand, 'Okay Mum, name some of your favourite authors, and tell me why you read them.'

'Well you know most of them'. I am feeling a bit put on the spot by her query, but try to answer her question. 'I've always loved Margaret Atwood, Alice Munro and Carol Shields for their depiction of women and their lives, and

Fay Weldon's quirky humour and Elizabeth Jolly's darkly wicked character, but I suppose they're all old-fashioned now and probably should be withdrawn.'

'No Mum, they shouldn't. They're still being read by my generation so should be kept. But those older writers are only part of this weeding programme. Novels by younger authors that depict women as self-motivated and freethinking are being removed, and in the non-fiction collection most of the books written by or about women are being withdrawn. All books that show women as intelligent, capable or creative are being removed.'

Fiona had talked to me the previous week about the planned weeding programme, so I still don't quite understand why she is so upset. I think she might be over-reacting and say, 'But darling weren't the staff told last week that most of the withdrawn items would be put on disc to ensure that they remain a viable part of the collection?'

She slumps back into a chair, 'That's what we were told, but today I went to the ground floor that leads to the loading bay. It was full of boxes, and they were all addressed to the Disposal Centre. They're not recording these books, but sending them straight to the furnaces. I opened one of the boxes and it contained biographies and autobiographies of women. The next one I opened was full of what I consider to be good fiction, and all written by women. Just as I was going to open a third box Mr. Aziz appeared, and asked me what I was doing. I just turned to him and said, 'I think you know,' then walked past him up the stairs. Later that day he came up to me and said he wants to see me in his office first thing tomorrow morning. I'm scared Mum. There's no-one in authority who I can tell about what's happening who will care, and

Joe's away working on a solar energy installation in Central Australia.'

As she says this she bursts into tears, and now I can hold her and stroke her back until she stops crying.

I am at a loss as to what Fiona can do. Our society has become so regimented and male-dominated I can't think of a useful suggestion, so take the easy way out.

I say, 'I suppose Mr. Aziz will query you about what you saw, so just act dumb. Say you were curious about what was in the boxes and apologise. If you want to keep your job don't let on about your suspicions and don't make waves.'

What cowardly advice I give my beautiful daughter and how I will come to regret it later. By my passive response Fiona knows I won't be an ally if she chooses to fight.

The next day Fiona dashes in with the children. When I try to ask her what she is going to do about the situation at work she brushes me off with, 'Must rush, I'm running a bit late.'

She kisses the children goodbye and is out the door in a flash.

That night she doesn't come back at the usual time to collect the children. I ring the library to see if she is working back, but get an answering machine message saying the library is closed and to ring again in the morning.

Bill is playing in the garden with Joanna and little Thomas and hasn't realised what the time is. When I tell him I am getting worried he says, 'She's probably just stopped to do a bit of shopping,' but I see a look of concern in his eyes for I had told him about what happened at the library the previous day.

He picks up Thomas and brings the children inside.

'Have we got the phone number for that friend of hers at work, Stephanie someone?' he asks.

Joanna, with that ability children have of sensing when something is wrong in their world, looks from Bill to me and asks, 'When's Mummy coming home?'

I desperately try to think of Stephanie's surname while Bill settles the children at the table with drinks of juice and cookies. The name Henderson pops into my head and, with trembling hands, I search the phone book for an S. Henderson. I feel panic rising in me as I place the call.

She answers at the second ring, and I barely have time to identify myself before she interrupts, 'Oh! Mrs. Harper, I've been sitting here wondering if I should call you. Soon after we started work today Fiona was called into Mr. Aziz's office, and she didn't come back. Later in the morning he told the supervisor Fiona had gone home sick, and that the roster would need to be rearranged to cover her absence. I thought it was odd because she hadn't said anything to me about feeling sick. I rang her as soon as I got home, but there was no answer. I've been so worried, but I haven't known what to do.'

Bill has been chatting to the children, but I know he has been listening because as soon as I'd thank Stephanie and hang up he looks at me, a query in his eyes.

'She left work this morning, supposedly because she was feeling ill, but Stephanie didn't see her after she was called to Mr. Aziz's office. I'm worried Bill. What can we do?'

He jumps up from the table saying, 'I'm ringing that fellow to find out what's going on. Pass me the phone book and I'll find his number.'

I hand it over to him with trembling hands. Both children are now looking worried and Thomas begins to cry.

Bill says, 'I'll make the call in the other room,' and leaves taking the book and phone with him.

I pick up Thomas and talked nonsensically about big boys not crying. I feel like crying myself.

When Bill comes back to the kitchen he is white. 'She's been taken to the Educational Institute. I'm going down there to see what I can do.'

He grabs his coat and car keys and is out the door before I can say anything.

I tell the children Mummy has to work late so they will stay with me for the night. I cook their dinner, bathe them and read them a story before putting them to bed in the room we have set up for when they stay with us. I am frantically worried, but have to pretend that everything is normal so that the children won't get upset.

By the time Bill returns I am a nervous wreck. No one really knows what happens in that wretched place. People who have been there don't ever talk about what they have experienced, but they come out changed.

As soon as I hear the car pull up outside I race to the door hoping Bill will have Fiona with him, but he is alone.

He comes into the room looking haggard, and before I can ask him anything says, 'They told me Fiona had become upset at work and needed counselling. When I asked to see her they said she'd been given a sedative and was sleeping. They suggested I ring tomorrow to find out how she is progressing. Oh! Marion I don't know what we can do.'

I burst into tears and he holds me until I stop.

We try to ring Joe on his mobile, but can't make contact. Obviously he is working in an isolated area where he is out of range.

When we finally go to bed, after spending the evening agonising over what might be happening to Fiona, we both toss and turn and get very little sleep.

The next day Bill doesn't go to work, but instead makes an appointment to see our lawyer. I can't go with him because I have the children to look after. The morning drags as I play with the little ones. All the time I am worrying and wondering about what is happening to our daughter.

I am nearly mad with worry by the time Bill returns in the afternoon. Thomas is having a nap and Joanna is watching television, so we can talk without them getting upset.

Over a cup of tea Bill tells me that the lawyer said there is nothing he can do to help us. He said that people taken to the Education Institute are not considered to be in need of legal representation because they are merely undergoing counselling to help them adjust to situations with which they aren't coping.

Bill had also been back to the Institute, but was once more refused permission to see Fiona. 'They were very polite, but said she needed time to make the necessary adjustments. When I asked what these so-called adjustments might be the fellow told me that my daughter was suffering from a serious delusion connected with her work, and needed help if she were to continue to hold down her job.' His shoulders slump and I see tears in his eyes as he continues, 'I don't know what to do. I feel so helpless.'

We sit in silence, sipping our tea and holding hands across the table.

Later we try again to phone Joe but still can't contact him, so we send him an urgent telegram asking him to get in touch with us.

On the fourth day they allow us to see Fiona. I am shocked by the rapid change in her. She has always been slim, but elegantly so. Now she looks positively skinny, and the grey shift she is wearing hangs loosely on her tall frame.

We sit in a small room that contains only a table and four chairs. An attendant is seated near the door, and watches us all the time.

Fiona's first words to us are. 'How are my babies? What have you told them about me not coming home?'

We reassure her about the children as well as we can, and then she asks, 'Have you been able to get in touch with Joe? Does he know I'm in here?'

We tell her about the problems we've had contacting Joe, and that he has finally received our telegram and rung us, but is having difficulties getting a flight back. Eventually we get a chance to ask her how she is feeling, if she is eating all right and if she has been mistreated.

She answers evasively. 'No, I'm not being mistreated. Yes, I am eating okay and sleeping all right.'

We don't believe her, for her eyes slide to the attendant at the door after each answer. I sense her fear.

After seven days in detention she returns home "re-educated".

Joe arrives in time to pick her up from the Institute, and we take the children back to their own house so that they are there to welcome her home.

She hugs us all, then sits down in a chair with Thomas on her lap and falls asleep.

During the first few days after she is freed from detention Fiona sleeps. She gets up in the morning and eats breakfast with Joe and the kids, but soon after she drops off to sleep in a chair, often with one of the children clasped firmly to her breasts.

Thomas usually stays there, glorying in the fact that he has his Mummy back, but Joanna soon slides from her grasp and asks crossly, 'Why's Mummy always sleeping now?'

Joe applies for and is given a fortnight's leave to look after his wife and children, but I go to their place every day to help out. Despite loving enquiries on his part Joe hasn't been able to find out from Fiona what happened to her at the Institute. He tells me that whenever he questions her she'd just say, 'I don't want to talk about it.'

The poor man is at his wit's end about how to help her.

On the third day he suggests that she might find it easier to talk to me about it, and takes the children off to a park to give us some time alone.

Fiona is napping in an armchair so I make us a cup of tea and wake her gently.

She stretches and reaches for her cup saying, 'Gosh I'm so damn tired all the time. You'd think I'd have caught up by now.'

Seeing this as an opening I ask, 'Didn't they let you sleep in there? What did they do to you my Darling?'

She looks close to tears. 'I really can't talk about it Mum. I know that Joe and you and Dad want to know, but so much of it is a blur, and even thinking about it and trying to remember gives me a headache.'

'Talking about it might help though. Get it out of your system.' I say tentatively, not wanting to put pressure on her while she is still in such an obviously fragile state.

She answers abruptly, 'Look Mum, I've told you most of it's a blur. I know I was cold and hungry, and that every time I started to go to sleep I'd be woken up again. I think they might've used some sort of drugs on me too because I have a vague memory of being injected with a needle. But I'm not sure. I'm not sure about anything anymore.'

With this she bursts into tears, and I feel dreadful for causing her distress when she has obviously suffered so much.

Later in the day, while Fiona is having an afternoon nap with Thomas and Joanna is watching television, I repeat this conversation to Joe.

He looks so upset and says, 'I hate the thought of leaving her while she's still so traumatised, but I've only been able to get two weeks off, and I really need to get back. Islanders are doing most of the work on this job with men from the National Militia as overseers. Freddy Fielding, my second in charge, is the only other professional out there, and although he knows his stuff he's not good with the men. I'm afraid he might turn a blind eye to the bullying those militia men get up to if you don't keep a close watch on them.'

I love Joe and can see how torn he's feeling. I suggest that he take Fiona away to somewhere really glamorous and luxurious for the weekend while we mind the children. This idea cheers him up a bit, and I am glad when

Fiona readily agrees to the suggestion. I had feared that she mightn't be willing to leave the children after her previous enforced separation from them.

Bill and the children and I wave them off happily on the Friday, and when they return on Sunday evening Fiona looks almost her old self. She raves about what a wonderful time they'd had with scrumptious meals, hot spas, soothing massages and wonderful walks in the rain forest.

The next day Joe is flying out early and Fiona is going back to work, so we all go to the airport.

She clings to Joe for a long time and I hear her say, 'I wish you didn't have to go,' but she waves him off with a smile, and chats quite happily about returning to work as we drive away from the airport.

I am anxious about how her first day back at work will go. The children and I bake a cake so that they can give their Mummy a nice surprise when she comes to collect them.

As soon as she walks in the door I know there have been problems, but I can't ask her about them while the children are around.

Later that evening I ring her when I know the children will be in bed. I ask her if everything had been all right at work.

She answers offhandedly. 'Okay, I guess. Mr. Aziz welcomed me back in that smarmy way he has, and all of the women asked me how I was feeling, but there's an odd atmosphere about the place. Everyone seems to be wary of being alone with me, and some have given me funny looks. I get the feeling they've been told I'd had some sort of breakdown.'

I say something neutral like, 'I guess things will soon settle down.'

We chat about what Bill and I plan to do with the children the next day and then we say goodnight.

For the next couple of days things seem to be normal. Fiona comes in and we chat over a cup of tea before she takes the children home.

On the Thursday, as soon as she walks in the door, I know something is wrong.

She looks pale and tense and when she has sat down she says, 'Something happened today Mum, and I think you can help me with it.'

I turn from pouring water into the teapot, slightly mystified by the serious tone in her voice, 'You know I'll do anything I can darling. What's the problem?'

While I pour our tea she says, 'Now don't think I'm being weird, but today I had to go down into the basement to get some request forms from the stationery cupboard. I was standing at the top of the stairs when suddenly I became dizzy. My head started pounding, and I could hear your voice saying very clearly "Don't make waves." What happened before I went to the Institute Mum? I feel I'm on the verge of remembering something important that I've forgotten, and I think you might know what it is.'

I don't know what was done to my beloved daughter in that awful place, but I don't want her to be sent back there again. Should I remind her about the boxes of books she had seen ready for destruction in the furnaces?

I sidestep her question by saying, 'You disagreed with part of the library's weeding policy, and I think I probably advised you not to make waves. Things are all right now at work aren't they?'

'I guess so. The range of our stock is very limited, but we've received a whole new lot of romances and cooking and craft books so the shelves are almost full again. There are so many gaps in the collection though. We have no biographies or autobiographies, very few art books, nothing on history or sport and certainly no literary fiction. I've been surprised that we've had very few complaints.

I feel relieved that Fiona seems to be going along with the changes; that somehow what was done to her at that place has given her an acceptance of the society in which we are now living.

I misjudged my daughter.

The next evening, when she comes to collect the children, she seems almost light-hearted. While we pack up the children's gear I ask her if they are coming to lunch on Sunday. She and the children often join us when Joe is away.

'No thanks Mum,' she says offhandedly, 'I ran into Phoebe today, and she and some of the other girls who were at university with us are coming around in the afternoon.'

As she is going out the door she turns and gives me a hug and whispers, 'I've remembered Mum. It all came back to me last night in bed, but you don't have to worry.'

The following week is much the same as usual, except that Fiona asks if we will keep the children with us on Wednesday night as she is meeting up with Phoebe and some of their other university friends again. I don't think anything of this because the kids often stay overnight with us when Joe is home and they are going out to dinner.

The next day Fiona has a sparkle about her that I haven't seen in weeks. My first thought is that perhaps she is having an affair, but this seems unlikely to me. She and Joe appear to be as much in love still as when they first met, despite the many months they spend apart because of Joe's work.

While we sip our tea I ask casually, 'Did you have a good night out with the girls?'

I can see she is holding something back. She has the same look on her face as she'd have as a little girl when she'd done something very good or very bad, and was not quite sure how to break the news.

Half- jokingly I ask, 'What are you lot cooking up? It wasn't just a normal night out with the girls, was it?'

She looks at me earnestly and says, 'You're not allowed to breathe a word of this, not even to Dad. Promise?'

I agree and she continues, 'We're putting together a newspaper, and we're all writing an article on what has happened to us in the workplace. There's Justine, who was a top surgeon and is now only allowed to practice obstetrics, and Anne who was a criminal lawyer and has been demoted to conveyancing. Phyllis was a presenter on a current affairs programme, but she was sacked because she queried the veracity of too many stories. A couple of the women were teachers and they lost their jobs because they complained about the curriculum they were meant to follow the way you did Mum.'

When she pauses briefly I stammer, 'But what do you hope to gain from producing this newspaper? And how are you going to print and distribute it? You'll all finish up in trouble.'

Fiona tosses back her hair and gazes at me intently, 'You've become so negative. Don't you see we have to do something? All women are becoming second-class citizens, and many of the less educated men are working under very poor conditions. No one speaks out for fear of being taken to the Education Institute or, worse still, the Correctional Institute. It's illegal to protest, and unions and federations are just about non-existent. One woman in our group, Sara, was a union representative, but they were virtually made redundant because the employers offered higher wages to non-union members. Now most workers have lost benefits they had previously. Sick leave is limited, holiday leave has been cut back to two weeks a year and overtime is unpaid. Sara says many of the factory workers are treated quite brutally by the members of the Militia who act as overseers.'

'I know there are a lot of things wrong in this New Australia of ours, but what do you hope to achieve with this newspaper?'

'Firstly we want to reach people who have experienced injustices in the workplace, to stop them feeling so alone by sharing our experiences with them. Secondly we hope to create a groundswell against the regimentation that's being inflicted on so many in our society. Before Raman and his New Australia Party we were an almost classless society, and now we've become an autocracy run by wealthy Muslim, Chinese and Indian men and a few wealthy Old Australians. Below them are the less educated Old Australians men, the Islanders and the Aboriginals and at the bottom of the pile are all women. If something isn't done it'll only get worse.'

'I know how you feel, but I worry that you'll get into trouble. I couldn't bear you being taken to that place again.'

She gives me a hug, 'Don't worry Mum. The printing press is well hidden in someone's basement, and we'll distribute the papers at night. Just remember don't even tell Dad about this. The only way we'll get caught is if someone blabs.'

Of course I worry, and it is very hard not to share the secret with Bill, but I keep my word.

Somehow they must have been discovered, because as soon as the first edition begins circulating Phoebe is run over by a hit and run driver, Sara supposedly commits suicide, and Fiona dies when according to later court evidence she trips at the top of the stairs leading to the basement and falls and breaks her neck.

We are told her death is the result of a terrible accident, but I know in my heart and my gut that what has occurred was not accidental. I know my girl has been murdered.

On the day it happens I am playing with the children in the back garden. It is bright and sunny, the first really warm day of the summer, and Bill and I have filled the paddle pool only this morning. Joanna is cavorting around in the middle of the pool, pretending to be a mermaid, while little Thomas plays at one side pouring water from one bucket to the other with the concentration of a scientist at work on an important experiment.

I am sitting in a canvas chair, eyes closed and enjoying the feeling of warmth on my face and arms when I become aware of a shadow blocking the sun. I open my eyes to see Bill and a black uniformed militiaman standing in front of me. I hadn't heard their footsteps across the grass and am at first merely startled by the sudden intrusion, but then I see the look on Bill's face.

'What's happened?' I shriek, panic causing my heart to thump and my voice to quiver.

Bill bends down and puts his arms around my shoulders, 'Fiona's dead. She died at work an hour ago. This officer has come to take us to the morgue so that we can officially identify her.' A great sob shakes his body and I cling to him, silenced by disbelief and shock.

When I can breathe again I stammer, 'But how? Where did it happen? What was she doing?'

The officer just stands there looking rather like an imposing black statue, his face hard and expressionless.

The sun glints off the dark glasses that hide his eyes as he answers in a deep, toneless voice, 'I'm not at liberty to discuss the event, but you will be given information about the demise of your daughter by officials at the Bureau.'

In my near hysterical state it occurs to me that he sounds like a robot from an old-fashioned movie, and this adds to the unreality of the situation. I just can't take in what I am being told.

I feel like sitting there like a dummy but Bill pulls me to my feet and whispers, 'Can you get Amy over to mind the kids? I don't think I can do this on my own.'

With tears streaming down my face I rush next door, and when Amy answers my loud knocking I fall into her arms and try to tell her what has happened. She holds me close and wipes away my tears, before leading me back to my place and assuring me she will take care of the children. Bill and I are then bundled into the back seat of the long, black car where we hold each other on that tense and seemingly endless journey.

I had seen my grandparents and my father after they died, and each time had been shocked by the change that occurs once the heart stops pumping and the brain closes down. They had all looked so different from when they were alive, more like waxen effigies than people.

Perhaps we do have a spirit that departs the body after death, leaving behind an empty cocoon.

Though it had been shocking to see these beloved people in death, I am unprepared for the horror I experience when I look at my Fiona lying on a slab. She is covered with a green sheet that the attendant pulls back so we can see her face and shoulders.

Her beautiful nose has been smashed and lies sideways onto one cheek. Huge black and purple bruises surround her closed eyes, and her mouth is set in a grim line. There is dark bruising on her neck and shoulders. I turn away, hardly able to breathe or take in the horror of it. I hear a harsh, keening sound filling the echoing room and realise that this strange noise is coming from me. I feel a strong arm across my back and then everything goes black.

For the first few days after Fiona's death I live in a sedated world.

I have memories of Jill being there, her face swollen and tearful, of Bill standing over me with a cup of tea almost begging me to drink it, of Joe bearded and travel-weary trying to hold me while I accuse him of neglecting my daughter by being away so much when she needed him to look out for her.

On the day of the funeral I must be only mildly sedated because I remember that clearly. I remember driving in a big black car with Bill next to the driver, and Joe and me in the back with the two children. I remember the short service, and the long time standing out the front of the funeral house while people, both familiar and unknown, hold my hand or hug me as they express their sympathy. I will never forget the burial, and the sight of Joe and the children holding hands, and then each throwing a rose onto the coffin as it is being lowered into the gaping hole.

For the next few weeks I stumble through the days, trying to get some order back into my life, trying to live with the reality that I will never again see my Fiona, never again watch her playing with the children, never again share with her a cup of tea; never again hold her in my arms.

I am plagued by nightmares that wake me hot and trembling in the night.

It's weird how the brain takes something and twists and turns it almost out of recognition. In this case my feelings of grief, and guilt that I should have tried to talk Fiona out of her involvement with the paper, become a different world of horror.

In one nightmare, that I have again and again, I am back in the days of the Mothers' Group before the fathers started joining us for picnics and barbecues. We eight mothers are at a park with our first babies. The kids are all about eighteen months old, and they are toddling around together under the trees or playing on a small slide while we women set out the lunch. We are talking and laughing together when suddenly a group of men enters the park. They are dressed in the black leather uniforms of the Militia, and as they march towards us their feet crunch noisily along the path. They stop in unison then the leader comes towards us across the grass.

I stand and say, 'Can we help you?'

He answers abruptly, 'It has come to the attention of the authorities that some of you women are not taking proper care of your children. I have orders to take the following children from you and place them in more responsible care.'

He then proceeds to read out four names including my Fiona and Ruth's Phoebe. Somehow the soldiers know who the named children are because they advance on them and pick up the four specified on the list. We mothers scream at the men to release our little ones, but when I try to pull my terrified daughter from the arms of the man holding her another man pushes me away roughly and I fall to the ground. The other three mothers whose children are being taken react in the same way but are also thrust aside. Amid screams from the terrified children the militiamen reform into their previous formation and begin marching out of the park. I stagger to my feet and begin to run frantically after the men begging and pleading with them to release the children, but I can't seem to catch up with them. They are getting further and further away and I watch in despair as Fiona struggles in the arms of a black-clad soldier.

I wake with my heart pounding, tears streaming down my face and my doona twisted around me so tightly I can barely move.

I straighten the doona and, as my heart slowly calms, drift off to sleep again.

Suddenly I am back in the park with the Mothers' Group and our little children are toddling together under the trees or playing on a small slide. I know something awful is going to happen, and I try to get the other mothers to pick up their children and leave the park, but they don't want to. I begin pleading with them to come with me, to escape before it is too late, but then I'd see the militiamen entering the park. I scream at the others to run, and then wake making a low, gasping sound.

Once more my heart is pounding and tears are streaming down my face.

I become frightened of going to sleep and stay up, wandering aimlessly around the house until eventually I curl up in an armchair and sleep from sheer exhaustion.

In my grief I shut myself off from Bill's offers of comfort, and behave coolly towards Joe when he brings the children around to see me.

One day, when he is visiting, Bill takes the children outside and Joe sits me down in the kitchen and says, 'We have to talk Marion. Since Fiona died you've treated me like some stranger you can't stand to have around. I love you and Bill, and it's killing me the way you're behaving. I know how much you loved Fiona but I loved her too.' He pauses and I hear a sob in his voice as he continues. 'She was my life, my reason for living and you're acting as if it's my fault that she died.'

He puts his face in his hands and I watch as tears filtered through his long, brown fingers and dampen the tablecloth. I stand, move around the table, hold him while he cries and say, 'I'm sorry I've been so hard on you. I know I've been unfair, but I can't help feeling that if you'd been here she mightn't have gotten involved with that paper, and even if she had they mightn't have dared do what they did to her.'

Joe looks at me baffled, 'I don't know what you're talking about Marion. What paper and who are they?'

Obviously Fiona had not talked to Joe about her group and what they planned to do. I tell him about it, and of how three of their group died within a week of each other, and that I am convinced their deaths are connected to what they were doing.

'God, I can see now why you've been so angry with me. I just accepted that it was an accident, but if you're right Fiona may have been murdered. I'm going to insist on a coronial enquiry, and see if a good lawyer can uncover anything suspicious.'

It is several months before the enquiry is finally held. At least there is still some semblance of a judicial system but, even so, Joe has to be very persistent to get the hearing. He hires a very good lawyer, an Old Australian named Todd Williams, who has a reputation for getting justice for clients fighting the establishment.

I go with Joe when we brief him.

After introductions are completed and we are seated Todd says cautiously, 'Now my understanding from what Joe has told me is that you think there were suspicious circumstances surrounding the death of your daughter. That you don't think it was an accident.'

Although I still feel I am breaking a confidence I tell Todd about the paper on which Fiona and the others had been working, and how two others in the group also died that week.

Todd listens closely as I am speaking and then says, 'I can see how this provides a motive for the possible murder of your daughter and why you're suspicious, but all this would be inadmissible at a coronial enquiry. What we need is evidence that Fiona's injuries weren't consistent with her falling down a flight of stairs. We'll have to get a copy of the medical report before we proceed.'

On our next visit Todd has a copy of the report, which he hands to us saying, 'It appears from this that Fiona's injuries and subsequent death were consistent with her having fallen.'

I run my eyes down the brief report: black eyes, smashed nose and broken neck. There is no mention of the quite extensive bruising on her neck. I turn to Joe, 'There's no mention of how badly her neck and shoulders were bruised. I remember wondering how that had happened.'

Joe looks baffled, 'I didn't see her until after the funeral staff had worked on her. They had patched up her nose and covered the bruising around her eyes somehow. She looked beautiful, but like a statue.'

He gives a great gulping sob and puts his head in his hands.

Todd looks across the desk at us, a genuine look of sympathy in his warm brown eyes, 'Look, I know how hard this is for you both, but this is vitally important. Severe bruising on the neck and shoulders would not have been caused by that fall, and the fact that it's not mentioned in the report is suspicious. The problem is that Joe can't back you up, so it would be your word against what's written in the report.'

'Bill was with me. We both went to identify her. He saw the bruising too and shares my suspicions. He will also testify that this report is incorrect.'

I say this with more confidence than I feel, for since Fiona's death Bill has aged tremendously and has sunk into a deep depression.

He is forever saying things like, 'I should have been able to protect my little girl,' and 'I wasn't any use to you either, when you were made redundant.'

I hand the report back to Todd, and he rereads it before saying slowly, 'But it will still be your word against the examining doctor. I'll have to see if I can cast any doubts about the thoroughness of his report before I decide whether or not to call you or your husband. Now is there anything else we can introduce that would cast doubts on the story that your daughter tripped and fell? The accident report says there was a small hole in the carpet at the top of the stairs, and that she must have caught the heel of her shoe in it.'

I pounce delightedly on this piece of information, 'Fiona never wore high heeled shoes to work. Because she was on her feet for a large part of the day she always wore flat heeled shoes to work, and they wouldn't be likely to catch in a small hole.'

Todd looks closely at the photographs accompanying the accident report and then says smiling, 'I think that fact is important because this photograph shows a very small, round hole that would only catch a thin heel. This may be the lynch-pin I can use to get the case reopened.'

We leave Todd's office feeling confident that if anyone can get to the truth of how Fiona died it is this clever young man.

Bill and I have never been into a law court before, and feel quite overwhelmed by the formality of the place. There is a raised dais in the front of the room, then an expanse of flooring with a desk and chairs on either side. Behind these desks are rows of connected tiered seating.

Bill and I are ushered into the room by a member of the militia and seated in the row directly behind the right-hand desk where we can see Todd, already seated and checking some papers on the desk. He turns and smiles at us briefly, and then we are all required to stand while the coroner enters the room and takes his seat on the dais.

The first witness called is the doctor, and he gives his evidence in a dry, factual voice.

I feel sick as he describes Fiona's injuries. Todd had warned me this would be hard on Joe and Bill and me, but I'm still not prepared for the extent to which hearing this affects me. Once again I see her lying on that slab, her beautiful face smashed and bruised. I feel bile rise up from my stomach and into my mouth. I try to get up from the seat before I vomit, but feel a controlling hand on my shoulder.

'I'm going to be sick.' I whisper desperately.

Todd, hearing my voice, turns then stands and asks permission from the court for me to leave, as I am feeling unwell.

The militiaman accompanies me outside, and I head straight for the women's toilet and am thoroughly sick. I have several drinks of water before leaving the toilet.

Bill and Todd are standing in the passage, obviously waiting for me to return.

When I join them Todd says, 'The coroner called a short recess after I finished cross-examining the doctor because I said I needed to consult with you. Doctor Jones was insistent that there was no bruising on the neck, and that Fiona's injuries were consistent with her having fallen. I can't see any way we can refute his testimony, so we'll have to focus on how it happened.'

After the short recess Mr. Aziz is called to the stand. I know from what Fiona had told me about this man I would not like him, but I am unprepared for the overwhelming sense of loathing that wells up in me at the sight of him. From the beginning I had thought he was connected in some way with the death of my daughter, and looking at him I am sure.

After he has verified his name and position at the library his lawyer asks him to describe the events of the day.

Aziz speaks slowly and ponderously in a heavily accented voice, 'The day was as normal. There had been a staff meeting in the morning, and then I had gone to my office to deal with some paperwork. At about twelve-thirty Miss Henderson burst into my room screaming that Mrs. Edgerton had fallen down the stairs and was dead. She was so hysterical it took a while before I understood what she was saying.'

'What did you do once you realised?'

'I immediately went to the stairs and could see Mrs. Edgerton lying at the bottom. It was obvious from the angle of her neck that she would be dead, but I checked her pulse just to be sure then told Carl, who is our delivery man and had followed me down, to ring the Militia and an ambulance.'

'What happened after they arrived?"

"The paramedic verified she was dead and contacted their base with that information. They were informed that they could not remove the body until after members of the Militia had examined the scene. When the Militia arrived they took photographs of the accident scene and talked to all staff members. They were trying to find out if anyone had seen what had happened, but no-one was near that part of the building at that time.'

'Did you form any conclusion at the time as to how the accident happened?'

'I didn't personally, but one of the officers showed me a small hole in the carpet at the top of the stairs and indicated that he thought this may have caused Mrs. Edgerton to trip.'

When it is Todd's turn to question Mr. Aziz he is very thorough. Obviously he shares our conviction that Mr. Aziz was connected to Fiona's death, and he questions him closely about his movements that day.

'You say you were in your office from the time the staff meeting ended until Miss Henderson appeared in an hysterical state. Is that so?'

'Yes. I was busy with paperwork.'

'Where is your office in relation to the stairs?'

'My office is situated over the basement so my door is a few metres along the passage from the stairs.'

'Was anyone else working in that area during the morning Mrs. Edgerton died?'

'There are other offices in that part of the building, but all of the other staff members were busy in the library except for Carl who had been working in the basement.'

'Where was Carl at the time of the accident?'

'He had deliveries in the morning, and he checked in with me shortly before twelve to see if I wanted him to buy my lunch while he was on his break. He returned shortly after the ambulance arrived.'

'Didn't you tell the court earlier that Carl followed you down and rang the ambulance?'

I feel my heart leap. Todd has caught Aziz lying about Carl's whereabouts on the day and this is suspicious.

Mr. Aziz frowns, 'Did I say that? It's so long ago, but yes, I do remember now. He wasn't back. It must have been someone else who rang the ambulance.'

'So there was no-one except you in that part of the building when Mrs. Edgerton died?'

At this stage the other lawyer objects and the coroner upholds the objection, but Todd has made the important points that Mr. Aziz or Carl could have been involved if the fall was not accidental. The whereabouts of Carl at the time of Fiona's death has not been properly verified, and I feel sure that he killed her under instructions from Mr. Aziz. I feel such a loathing for both men and find it hard to sit passively while the questioning continues.

Todd picks up the accident report and says 'This report states that there was a small hole in the carpet at the top of the stairs. Did you notice this at the time of the accident?'

Aziz, looking slightly flustered answers, 'As I have already said I hadn't, but the Militia officer pointed it out to me.'

'Did you think that this could have caused Mrs. Edgerton to fall?'

'The officer thought this was the likely cause and it seemed reasonable to me. The young ladies wear such silly shoes with thin, high heels that could easily catch in such a hole.'

'Was Mrs. Edgerton wearing "silly shoes" with thin heels?'

'I cannot say that I noticed, but I assumed she must have been from what the officer said.'

I am expecting Todd to question Mr. Aziz further at that point, but he simply thanks him and sits down.

The next witness called is Stephanie Henderson. She appears agitated and nervous, and answers the questions put to her by the other lawyer in a voice that is so soft I have to listen closely to hear her. She tells how she had been going to Fiona's office to discuss a display they were planning to set up in the library. She saw her friend's body lying at the bottom of the stairs, had stumbled down to look closer, and then run screaming to Mr. Aziz's office.

Todd begins his questioning very gently. 'You and the deceased were close friends?'

'Yes, we had worked together before she went on maternity leave and when she came back.'

'I know that this is hard for you, but what injuries did you notice when you saw your friend lying at the bottom of the stairs?'

'Her head was twisted so much I knew her neck must be broken. I knew she must be dead.'

'Did you notice any other injuries, bruising to her neck and shoulders, for instance?'

'I noticed her face of course. She'd been beautiful you know, but her face was shattered. Her nose was broken and there were great purple bruises around her eyes.' Stephanie shudders and begins to cry.

Todd waits while she wipes her eyes with a tissue and then he repeats, 'Did you notice any bruising on Mrs. Edgerton's neck and shoulders?'

'All I remember was that her neck was at an unnatural angle, and her face was shattered. It was devastating to see her like that.'

Once more Stephanie bursts into tears and Todd waits while she wipes away more tears before continuing.

'Do you remember what sort of shoes Mrs. Edgerton was wearing on the day of the accident?'

Without pause she answers, 'Fiona was so tall she usually preferred flat-heeled shoes, but I really don't remember what kind of shoes she was wearing that day.'

'Would she have been likely to trip on that small hole in the carpet in flat-heeled shoes?'

At this the other lawyer objects and says Todd is leading the witness and that it has not been ascertained what sort of shoes the deceased was wearing.

Before Todd can ask her any more questions Stephanie blurts out, 'I don't remember what sort of shoes she was wearing, but I don't think she tripped. It's more likely that she had another dizzy turn. She'd felt dizzy at the top of those stairs only a week or so before the accident, so I thought it had happened again.'

When I hear Stephanie blurt this out I see all hope fade of us getting a reopening of a hearing into the cause Fiona's death. Without meaning to, she has destroyed that chance. Todd verifies this when we meet during the brief recess.

He shrugs his shoulders and sighs, 'I'd had high hopes that what Miss Henderson had to say would show up the inconsistencies, but I'm afraid her evidence hasn't helped at all. She didn't notice any bruising to the neck, and her mentioning your daughter's dizzy turn makes the matter of whether she was wearing high–heeled shoes or flats irrelevant. I'm sorry, but I'm afraid the original finding of accidental death will be upheld.'

He is correct.

When we file back into the court we are informed by the coroner that there is insufficient new evidence to warrant a reopening of the case, and that he accepts the original verdict of accidental death.

I know our daughter was murdered, probably choked to death then thrown down the stairs by the elusive deliveryman Carl. I have no doubt that hateful slimy Mr. Aziz masterminded her death but we can't prove this. Bill, Joe and I leave the court knowing we have taken our search for justice as far as we can and failed.

Although initially Bill seemed to cope better than I with the terrible loss of our daughter, as the months pass he becomes more and more depressed. He refuses to return to work and is retired on invalidity superannuation.

During the months before the coronial enquiry was held he often spoke about the pointlessness in even trying to get justice in our society as it now is, but he must have had some hope. After it is over he sinks more deeply into depression.

The next few months are ghastly. Except for the horrible time after I was forced out of my job we had always been so close and able to communicate well. Now he withdraws into himself and sits for hours in our little library room gazing blindly up at the mountain. When I join him and try to get him to talk he says, 'I failed her. I didn't look after her the way a father should.'

It seems to me that because he feels he failed to take some necessary action that could have saved Fiona he is now wallowing in an orgy of self-loathing. I become impatient with his inertia, with his unwillingness to try to move on by helping Joe and me with the children but later I will come to see why our reactions were so different. Right now his behaviour simply annoys me.

From the time the girls were born we had seen our parenting roles as different. Although we shared many of the chores associated with caring for children I had felt I was the primary nurturer, probably because I breast fed them for their first months of life, and was at home with them during those early, important years. Bill had seen himself as the protector of his family, and obviously continued to feel this responsibility even after the girls married. Because of this he hadn't shared nor understood my anger towards Joe for being away when Fiona had needed him.

Now he often becomes angry with me and shouts, 'Why didn't you tell me about her getting involved with that group, putting herself in danger?'

Even though Fiona had told me in confidence about the paper she and her friends planned to produce Bill makes me feel guilty about keeping this from him, and I respond abruptly from this sense of guilt.

Soon we are living almost separate lives.

Joe has insisted on being based in town so that he can care for his children, but he still has to go to work. To make it easier for him I spend most days at their house instead of expecting him to bring them to ours. In this way I can mind the children, but also do the household chores and prepare the evening meal for them before going home to Bill.

I try to get him to come with me, but he can rarely be roused from his despondency so stays at home. As a result of what I see as his self-centred behaviour the children, who are missing their mother, now also see little of their grandfather. This is yet another cause of dissension between us.

I had often heard of couples separating after the death of a child or the birth of a mongoloid or autistic baby, and had never understood why this happened so frequently. To me it seemed logical that the shared misery should have brought them closer together in support of one another. What happens to Bill and me helps me understand better the dynamics of loss; of how different forms of grieving and of dealing with that grief can create an unbreachable chasm between previously close and loving couples.

Besides his depression and inertia, or perhaps because of them, Bill is now sleeping very badly. As a result he looks haggard and tired, and lacks the energy to do even the smallest physical task. Several times I try to get him to see a doctor but he says gruffly, 'Stop nagging me woman. I can look after myself.'

I get peeved about him speaking to me like this, and so the chasm widens.

Initially caring for the children is heartbreaking. They miss their mother so much. They know she has died, that her body is in the ground and her spirit has gone to Heaven, but they are too young to really understand.

At time Thomas forgets and says, 'When's Mummy coming home?'

Joanna gets angry with him and shouts, 'Stupid boy, she can't come back from Heaven.'

At this Thomas cries and often we all finish up in tears.

It is also so hard for Joe. He loved Fiona very much, and now regrets bitterly the amount of time they had spent apart during their marriage. He feels guilty about not having being around to protect her, and I find myself in the peculiar position of reassuring him about something of which I had actually accused him.

The healing is slow, but gradually the children learn to laugh again and this cheers up both Joe and me.

The year after Fiona died Joanna starts school, and comes home with new songs and games to share with her brother. Joe also books Thomas into one of the few remaining Childcare Centres two days a week to give me more time at home with Bill.

I know I have been neglecting him to a certain extent while I have busied myself with helping the children and Joe adjust to life without Fiona. Now I determine to try and get him to take an interest in living again.

I buy a new book about edible fungi and berries that can be found in our region, and encourage him to join me on walks up the mountain and into the hinterland. He comes with me, but often is unwilling to go as far as I want to, and I am surprised at how quickly he tires.

When we were young we did a lot of bushwalking, and this continued once the children were old enough to come with us. Always this had been something we enjoyed together, but now I feel I am bullying him into something that he really doesn't want to do.

I also try to get him interested in extending the vegetable garden and adding to the plantings in our large, sloping front area. He accompanies me on visits to the nurseries and later helps plant what we have bought, but he seems to do everything under sufferance and I become impatient with his lack of enthusiasm.

From the time of Fiona's death Bill insists on watching our leader's weekly talk to the nation. Raman commenced these talks back in the early forties, but after I recovered from my bout of depression, Bill and I steadfastly turned off the television when they were due to come on. We told each other we were not going to be manipulated and brainwashed further by this man.

Now Bill sits hunched over, staring at the set, muttering wildly at the figure on the screen. Initially I too watch, curious to learn about the current content of our leader's speeches.

In the few years since I had last seen him on the television screen Raman has changed. Whereas before he had presented a rather benign face to the world he now has the look of a fanatic, and in every speech he reiterates the message of how weak and dysfunctional the Old Australia had been. By shaming us is he softening us up for the introduction of even more draconian laws than those we already have?

These speeches make Bill so angry at time I fear for his sanity, but if I say anything he turns on me and says sneeringly, 'You voted for that animal. I always knew he wasn't to be trusted but you wouldn't listen to me. Now he's destroyed our country and made a society where innocent people are killed if they try to speak out against what's going on.'

I have no answer to his accusations because I had indeed been taken in by Raman, and not foreseen where his policies were taking us. All I can do now is beg Bill not to watch the programme as it upsets him so much, but he ignores me. It is as if by feeding his hatred in this way he assuages some of the guilt he is feeling.

He continues to sleep badly. I often wake in the night, and reach across to his side of the bed to find it cold and empty. Then I lie awake wondering what he is doing. Sometimes I get up and join him in the kitchen for a cup of tea, and then try to talk him back to bed. Often he refuses and I leave him, staring out at the blackness, and I think what a silly old fool he's become.

One night I wake alone as has become so usual, but I know something isn't right. There is no light filtering along the passage from the kitchen, and no sound of him shuffling around or talking to the cat. The house is absolutely silent and I feel an inexplicable sense of dread.

I jump from the bed and run down the passage calling his name. He is not in the kitchen or the lounge room, but then I see a crack of light under the library door.

He is sitting in the little armchair. On his lap is a small, tattered book that had been Fiona's favourite, but his eyes are closed. I call his name once more, and then go to him to encourage him back to bed, but he sits there still and cold and dead, his face still wet with tears.

When someone you love dies the worst thing that those who survive must live with are regrets. Of course the initial reactions are those of pain and loss. These feelings pass after weeks or months or even years, but the regrets last forever.

I still regret that I couldn't help Bill through that horrible year after Fiona died, that we so often angered each other when we did talk about it, and that I left him too much alone. He had been my love and my friend for nearly forty years, and I hadn't made enough effort to help him survive his sorrow and sense of failure.

My emotional state at this time is so complex and confusing, and different from the way I had felt after Fiona was killed.

When she died I was so totally overwhelmed by the sense of loss there was no room for any other emotion but sorrow.

With Bill's death I feel the full range. I alternate between feelings of sorrow, despair, anger and, at times, even a strange sense of relief that he is no longer feeling such misery. But most of all I feel guilty that I hadn't been able to pull him out of his depression; had not tried hard enough to help him want to go on living.

Because of these feelings of guilt I don't query so much of what happens to me shortly after the funeral.

The Friends visit me and while still in a state of shock and deep sorrow from the loss of Bill my life undergoes further dramatic changes.

I had heard vague rumours about this group who helped widows adjust to their changed circumstances but had no idea what these so-called Friends actually did. None of my friends or acquaintances has been widowed, so I hadn't really thought much about this, or of the ramifications of being a lone woman in this now male-dominated society. Why I didn't take more notice of these rumours I don't know, but because I hadn't I am totally unprepared for what is to come.

Before the Friends come Ali visits me and sits me down to discuss finances. When I lost my job my superannuation had gone into Bill's and my joint account. At that time the bank changed the account name to Bill's only. We thought this was odd and a bit unfair, but when we queried this we were told this was now bank policy. This hadn't bothered me unduly, because from the time of our marriage we had always shared our money and run a joint account. I wrongly assumed that should Bill die before me the account would simply be changed to my name.

Now my son-in-law sits across from me and explains how gradually all joint accounts were changed in this way, and now only a very few single women who are still working have control of their money.

Once more I feel what a fool I had been not to query what was going on in our current society, but until something affects one most people don't ask enough questions.

When I criticise myself for being so foolish Ali puts up his hand and shushes me. 'Mother Marion you couldn't be expected to think of this. You've been used to things being organised differently, but you needn't worry. I've applied for the account to be put into my name, and you will have access to it through me. If it's not in the name of a male relative it will be managed by the state, and that would be much more difficult for you.'

Of course I agree to his suggestion. Even though he can be dominating I think he is basically a good man and I would prefer to have him handle my money than the state.

I have since wondered though, why did I hand over this control to Ali? He was after all a member of what was the equivalent to the Master Race in Hitler's Germany. Why didn't I tell him I would prefer to have Joe handle the financial matters in my life? This would have been quite reasonable for at that time Joe and I were very close, having spent so much time together caring for the children.

Suffice to say I did give Ali that control, and he didn't let me down, well at least not for a long time. Considering the things that happened later I hate to think what would have happened to me if I'd relied on Joe.

A few days after my conversation with Ali I am contacted by the Civilian's Services Centre and told to expect a visit from the Friends, but am unsure what these so-called Friends will do. I'd have thought that, with the matter of finances settled, there would be no need for any further government interference in my life. I couldn't have been more wrong.

The group of Friends consists of two men and one woman. The man in charge of the group is of Middle-eastern extraction, and looks to be in his mid-forties.

The younger man is shy and nerdy-looking and still bears the marks of adolescent acne on his narrow face, while the young woman is quite startlingly attractive with vivid blue eyes and a wide, smiling mouth. By their accents and colouring I can tell that these two are Old Australians.

As I usher them into my home I wonder why they are here. I know from first-hand knowledge how the lives of women have become so restricted and have learnt from bitter experience what can happen to any woman who attempts to make demands for change. I have now been forced to face the fact that I no longer even have the right to access my own money without first consulting Ali. Knowing all this I really don't see how there can be any more changes that will impinge on my life. I am in for a shock.

After I invite the Friends into the lounge room I offer them tea or coffee, but the older man answers for the others, 'We have much to do so we'll decline your kind offer. I am Daoud Khalil and my two young helpers are Donald and Jennifer. We understand from your son-in-law that you don't wish to go to one of our many lovely retreats, so we must make your house safe for you to remain here.'

Completely bemused I stammer, 'What exactly does that entail? We already have a security system, and I have good locks on the doors.'

'Ah! You don't understand what I mean. Now that you are on your own it's not legal for you to have the same computer or telephone access you had previously. We must also check to ensure there are no books remaining in the house that are deemed unsuitable for a woman alone to have in her possession.'

I begin to say, 'This is absurd...'

Mr. Khalil silences me with a wave of his hand and says impatiently, 'Don't make things difficult for yourself and us. Unless you comply with what we must do you will be at risk of a visit from members of the Civilian Services Department, and then your son-in-law may not be able to protect you.'

Initially I am terrified and bewildered, and just sit on the couch watching as Donald fiddles with the computer and the telephone. When Mr. Khalil and Jennifer pass through the lounge each carrying a box of my books I regain some semblance of self-control, and walk to the library while they are packing the boxes in the car. Already my father's collection of history books is packed, and they have made a start on Bill's books.

When they return to the room I try to steady myself before demanding, 'What right have you to do this? These books are my personal possessions. What harm can come from my being allowed to keep them?'

Mr. Khalil looks at me with eyes as cold and hard as stone and says, 'Jennifer, take Mrs. Harper into the kitchen and make her a cup of tea.'

I want to run outside and call for help, to jump in our car and drive to Jill's place, to do anything but sit in the kitchen and drink tea, but that is exactly what I do. I feel as powerless as a rape victim must feel.

When I begin to cry Jennifer puts a tentative hand on my shoulder and says, 'Don't let it get you so upset Mrs. Harper. There are some lovely books in the libraries and some really good plays on the television.'

I look into her vivid blue eyes and see kindness and concern there, but not a trace of genuine understanding of what those books could possibly mean to me. In this lovely young woman I see the end result of what was deemed a "suitable" education for girls.

As they are leaving Mr. Khalil delivers the final blow with his off-hand comment, 'Someone will be along in the morning to collect your husband's car. It will be given a valuation, and the money for it will be put into the account that is now to be managed by your son-in-law.'

Although I have been feeling powerless to argue further this new bit of information stirs my anger and I shout, 'What do you mean my husband's car. We always shared the car and now it is mine. What are you talking about saying it will be taken away.'

He gives me a false smile as he says, 'surely you realise women are no longer allowed to own cars?

With a little shrug he continues, 'I don't think you realise how lucky you are Mrs. Harper to have such a caring man as your son-in-law in your family. Many widows are far worse off than you.'

As soon as they drive away I go into the library and see with dismay how few books still remain. My father's entire collection of history books has gone, along with all of Bill's books and most of mine. I have been left with a few works of fiction and the books on cooking, gardening, and natural history. My small collection of books on art have also been decimated. While they have left me with the books dealing with technical aspects of painting they have taken my much-treasured books about the works of Monet and Van Gogh that I bought in France many years ago. Missing are also three other particular favourites, Australian Art in the Twentieth Century, Artists of the Heidelberg School and a beautifully illustrated book of the life and works of Margaret Olley.

As is to be expected they have left me with a recent acquisition, "Islamic Art Through the Centuries." I had bought it to learn more about the history and culture of these people who are now dominating our country. In anger I throw the book across the room.

The only section they haven't touched is the small assortment of children's books. I sit on the floor clutching a copy of Alice in Wonderland.

When I was a child my father had read this book to me, and I in turn read it to Fiona and Jill. It is old and faded, but I have kept it to read to my grandchildren when they are old enough to understand it. Now I sit on the floor, feeling as confused as Alice had in the strange world in which she found herself. Unlike Alice I don't have the flexibility of youth on my side, and feel fearful of what else can happen to me in this strange and rapidly changing world.

I am still there when Jill and Ali arrive. She had known the Friends were going to make their visit, and has insisted on Ali bringing her to my place as soon as he arrived home from work.

I tell them what has happened, and while Jill makes us all strong cups of coffee Ali checks the computer and telephone. I am in for another shock.

While we sip our drinks Ali says, 'As I expected you now have limited computer access. It looks as if all they have left you with is the ability to listen to and download music and other forms of entertainment. You will also still be able to shop on line.'

'And the phone?'

'I don't think they've put a tap on it, but I'm pretty sure there will be limitations on who you will be able to call. You can probably only find out the extent of these limitations by calling people you normally would and seeing if you get through.'

I am still totally bewildered by the events of the day and can only ask, 'But why have they done this? What possible threat to society can I be if I have some books in my home and can access the limited information that is still available on the Internet? Or if I want to ring my friends and acquaintances?'

Ali looks decidedly uncomfortable as he begins, 'I don't think you realise how lucky you are Mother Marion...'

I interrupt impatiently, 'This has already been pointed out to me, and I'm grateful Ali for your help, but I still don't understand why any of this needed to be done.'

I know from certain things Jill has told me that Ali can have a short fuse, and I can see my questioning is beginning to annoy him.

He answer abruptly. 'You must understand that in our society the laws may sometimes seem unnecessarily strict or even grossly unfair, but they must be adhered to. You really are much better off than most widows believe me.

Now we must get back to our place. A neighbour is minding the girls and we need to let her go home.'

After they leave it is getting late, but I can't resist the urge to try ringing two of my closest friends. There is neither a ringing nor an engaged signal on either number. The lines are dead.

Before going to bed I return to the library and pick up from the floor the book on Islamic art. Slowly and carefully I tear it up, page-by-page, and then feed each one into the fire.

Are these the actions of a sane person? I think I am behaving quite rationally, for I consider that if the art of my country and that of France are to be censored I will censor the art of my oppressors. I feel a sense of satisfaction as I watch the highly decorated pages smoulder and flare colourfully until they disappear in the smoke.

During the next year I grieve for Bill. The last terrible year before his death haunts me, and somehow wipes away all the good times we had shared. I try to think of those joyous early years of our marriage, or of the times when the girls were little tots, and how we had watched them grow up to be beautiful young women.

Instead I dwell on all the bad times, my depression after I was made redundant, the horror of Fiona's death and the final despairing year of Bill and I living together but apart.

Having once succumbed to depression I fear being like that again, so try to fight the overwhelming blackness when it descends.

One thing that helps is being active, so I spend long hours in my garden planting, digging and weeding until exhaustion drives me indoors. Often after a day in the garden I sleep soundly through the night without the aid of a sleeping pill.

Slowly I begin to take an interest in living again, mainly because of the joy I gain from being with my grandchildren.

2051 – 2055

As I no longer have a car I catch the bus to Joe's house three times a week, and mind Thomas during the day then collect Joanna from school in the afternoon. These two little people are so sweet and bright and they give me the love and cuddles I so desperately need.

Once both children are at school all day I continue to collect them two or three days a week and I play with them, help Thomas with his home reader and then we cook the evening meal together. After dinner Joe and I bathe the children and they snuggle in the back seat of his car in their pyjamas when he drives me home.

Joe is a great father and as concerned as I about the limited education nine year-old Joanna has so far received. There is no comparison between what is being taught at her school and the boys' school Thomas is attending. To ensure Joanna doesn't miss out on the education a girl as intelligent as she deserves I get Joe to buy the same blocks and counting cards as those used in the boys' schools. Using these Joanna gains a reasonably good basic knowledge of mathematics. I also read to them from the extensive collection of books Joe has acquired, and play word games that improve the spelling and written skills of both children.

At least once a week I visit Jill and her ever-increasing brood. By now she has her three little girls, Sara, Amani and Fatima as well as Abdullah their treasured son and heir. The girls are sweet and gentle and Abdullah is an adorable, dark, curly-haired toddler who is fussed over and treated almost like a doll by his adoring sisters. Of course it is always a pleasure to spend time with Jill and I love her little ones, but the bond I share with Joanna and Thomas is stronger. I have spent far more time with them, and I guess I also feel they need me more. It's important to feel needed as you get older.

For the next year my life continues in this way and I gradually adjust to living alone, to not having the use of a car and to having limited access to money without consulting Ali. There are many things about our society I'm not happy about particularly the fact that Australian women have become second-rate citizens. Often I moan to Joe about what is happening and he agrees with me that things are so bad now for women and a lot of men. He doesn't think anything it is likely to happen to reverse this situation and thinks they could even get worse. I certainly couldn't imagine things becoming any worse in our society, but in this I am mistaken.

In 2051 Mohammed Raman suffers a massive stroke that leaves him severely handicapped and he dies soon after. His son, who at this time is about twenty-eight, takes over the leadership of the country. He immediately proclaims laws and regulations that are far harsher than any his father had brought in.

In his own twisted way Raman the First was a visionary who saw a need to drastically change Australian society if we were to survive as a nation almost in isolation. I think that initially segregation of schooling was aimed at providing a better education for both boys and girls. The high unemployment problem caused by a sudden influx of people, and later the necessity for Australia to become self-sufficient because of the isolation caused by disappearing oil reserves meant further changes needed to be made. Altering the kinds of education received by both boys and girls was supposedly aimed at solving some of these problems. Don't get me wrong. I still hate him for what happened to my small family under his rule, but I think he was initially prompted by a desire to create a workable society. He also seemed to have an almost paternalistic attitude towards women and under his rule there probably were retreats for elderly widows and lone women.

In contrast his son seems to feel only disdain for our sex.

Raman the Second, as he has chosen to be called, declares it compulsory for all women to wear brown cloaks with hoods at all times except within the privacy of our homes. This edict is undoubtedly because he grew up in a home where his mother continued to wear the burka but the reason given for the addition of hoods to our ugly brown capes is that hoods will provide us with protection from the lustful eyes of men.

Curfews are introduced, and only those male citizens with special permits are allowed out after eight in the evening. All group meetings are under surveillance, and anyone who dares voice the least opposition to the government disappears behind the walls of the Disposal Centre.

We Australian women had gradually accepted the wearing of our often rather plain home-made clothes but we had at least been allowed to experiment with natural dyes to bring some colour into our wardrobes. Now we must all wear brown when out in public and be covered from head to foot. The exceptions are the women employed by the government who all wear factory-made sky blue uniforms and the Madams who seem to be a law unto themselves. They have also been allowed to dress their girls and women in coloured clothing. The only ones of these imprisoned women we ever see are the Floozies, who are those who have chosen to be in this profession.

As mentioned earlier occasionally some of them are to be seen on the streets clad in red dresses and capes being escorted by a Madam to a special function for high ranking officers.

Another change Raman the Second introduces is the so-called ban on alcohol. This means that it becomes a punishable offence to consume any alcoholic drink. Most hotels close immediately and are changed into dormitory accommodation.

This law has a drastic effect on the wine and beer producers of the country. The smaller grape growers and vignerons face financial ruin, but some of the bigger ones continue to produce supposedly for the export market. It is said that those who are allowed to continue in business make generous contributions to the government's coffers as well as supplying wine to high up members of the hierarchy.

This Raman has the same good looks and charisma as his father, but he is far more arrogant and militant. Whereas Raman the First had appeared to be driven by a need to bring about changes that would, in his opinion, improve the country, his son seems to be driven by a lust for power and complete control. There is an old saying, 'Power corrupts and absolute power corrupts absolutely'. This is true in his case.

He makes it compulsory to listen to his weekly speech on television. Every household is issued with a device that is to be attached to the television set. By this means the viewing public can be monitored, and there are serious repercussions for those who do not tune in.

Under his leadership the law courts cease to function. People who are seen to flaunt the laws are dealt with in secret by members of the Internal Security Force and disappear into the Disposal Centre. The membership of the Militia Force is increased, and now these men are to be seen everywhere, patrolling the streets, outside the picture theatres and even at the beaches. They always travel in pairs and in their black leather uniforms, high boots and dark shades they are an ominous presence.

By this time, Joe is considered to be one of the country's experts in solar power installations. Because of this he has been informed that his services are required in Saudi Arabia where he is to oversee a gigantic installation in the dry desert area in the northeast of the country.

Shortly after being told about this move we are sitting in my kitchen having a cup of tea while the children watch a programme on television. He has seemed preoccupied all through dinner, so as soon as we are alone I ask him if anything is worrying him.

He answers, 'There's something important I want to ask you. I've checked with the department, and they've agreed to allow you to come with us if you will. They weren't too keen on the idea, but I pointed out how important you've been in the lives of my children since their mother died and that they'd need a familiar person around when I was away on site. Will you come?'

I feel quite taken aback and stammer, 'Gosh, I'd love to. I've been dreading the thought of not seeing the kids for a long time, but I don't know how I'd cope in a strange country. How long is your contract for?'

'Well my contract's for three years, but there's something else you need to know before you make your decision. We're not coming back.'

I must look totally shocked and bewildered because Joe reaches across the table and takes my hand before continuing, 'Once we get to Saudi I plan to defect to the United European Community. Others have done it so I know it's possible.'

'But Joe think of the risk. What will happen if you get caught?'

'It's worth the risk. Think of the life Joanna will have in this country. She's bright, as you know, but already she's slipping behind Thomas in maths. She's never going to be taught any of the sciences, or even know how to access computer information. She's only as knowledgeable as she is because of the time you've spent reading and talking to them both. But it's not only my concern about Joanna's education that's driving this decision. The other thing is I don't want Thomas growing up in this society, where women are treated like chattels and men are streamed into employment based on their ethnic background. No one is free, and it's only going to get worse. Raman the Second is a total megalomaniac and far worse than his father. I want a free and decent life for my kids. They're not going to get it in Australia but I've heard on the grapevine that things are going well in the United European Community. I'm positive you would be happier and have a better life if you'd come with us. It must be so frustrating for you not being allowed to own and drive a car or handle your finances or even decide what you wear.'

I had so frequently moaned to Joe about the restrictions I am now forced to put up with, so he knows how disgruntled I feel at times. It is sweet of him to think of this and to organize for me to go with them, but I am finding it all too much to consider.

In my confused state I babble, 'But I'd never see Jill and her little family ever again, and how do you know we'd be able to get away? What would happen if we were caught?'

Joe squeezes my hand, 'Look Marion, I know this is a big decision and you'll need some time to think it over. Of course you'll want to talk to Jill about going, but you mustn't tell her about my plan to defect. No one must know if we're to be safe. Let me know what you decide by next week, but please give it serious consideration. Since Fiona was killed you have been so important in the lives of Joanna and Thomas, and they'd miss you terribly if we have to go without you.'

After Joe and the children have gone home I go to bed, but lie awake for hours thinking about what Joe plans to do, and whether or not I will go with them. If I don't I will never see them again, and the thought of this is heartbreaking, but I am also saddened by the thought of never seeing Jill or my other grandchildren again. I am also fearful of what would happen if we were caught while defecting.

I finally fall asleep exhausted only to be haunted by a nightmare in which I am stumbling across an unending hot, dry desert with Joanna and Thomas who are both crying and thirsty. We are trying to find Joe, but he seems to have disappeared. I know we are being followed and that we won't be safe unless we can reach an oasis I can see in the distance. We trudge on and on but the oasis seems to remain as far away no matter how many sandy hills we climb. I feel an overwhelming sense of fear that I won't be able to get the children to safety.

I wake covered in sweat and with my heart racing so quickly I can hardly breathe.

The next day I ring Jill as soon as I am out of bed, and ask her to come and see me as I want to talk to her about something important, and I don't want to do it over the phone. She says she can get the gardener, who doubles as a chauffeur, to bring her as soon as she returns from walking the little girls to school. I shower and dress and am still finishing my breakfast when she arrives with Abdullah. At this time he is four and totally adorable with dark curly hair, big brown eyes and long, long lashes that only boy children seem to get.

As I hug him Jill says, 'This is unusual Mum. What's so important that you couldn't tell me about it on the phone?'

'Put the kettle on for another cup of tea while I settle Abdullah in the lounge and then we can talk.'

I bring out the box of toys I have collected for Joanna and Thomas to play with when I mind them at my place, and Abdullah immediately hones in on the blocks and begins building a tower. Basically he is a good little boy, although being the only son he is rather spoilt.

I join Jill at the kitchen table and she says, 'So what's the problem? You sounded a bit worried on the phone. Do you need money for something?'

'No it's nothing like that. Joe told me yesterday he and the children are going to Saudi Arabia on a three-year contract. He will be in charge of a large solar installation.'

'Oh Mum! You'll miss those two so much. You've been like a mother to them since Fiona died.'

She looks sad thinking about her lost sister. Fiona's death left an unfillable gap in Jill's life as it has in mine.

Before she can continue I interrupt, 'Well that's what I wanted to talk to you about. It's not only that they'll be gone for three years, but Joe's also arranged for me to go with them if I want to.'

A wary look crosses Jill's face but she just says, 'And?'

'I don't know whether I should go or not, so I wanted to talk to you about it. I know I'll miss Joanna and Thomas terribly if I don't go, but if I do I won't see you or your darling little girls and Abdullah for a long time.'

I want so much to say, 'It will be forever,' but know I mustn't.

In a sightly exasperated voice Jill says, 'Look Mum I know you favour Joanna and Thomas over my kids, and I guess that's only natural. You've spent so much more time with them, minding them when Fiona went back to work as well as more recently. At times I've felt a bit put out that you care more for them than for my little brood. I don't expect it's really much of a decision.'

She sounds slightly bitter so I hasten to add, 'But I'd miss you too my darling.'

'Not the way you miss Fiona. I know you never loved me as much as you loved her.'

I begin to say that this isn't true but Jill continues, 'It's okay Mum. I know that compared to Fiona I was always a bit of a wimp, and that you never respected or admired me in the same way you did her. But I'm not like she was. I've never had the courage to stand up for myself. I've let Ali decide everything and will probably continue to do so. I'm not a fighter like Fiona was.'

I am rather taken-a-back by this outburst from my gentle daughter.

I walk around the table and hug her, 'I am closer to Joanna and Thomas than to your children, but that's only because they've needed me more. As far as you and your sister are concerned I've always loved you just as much. I love your gentleness and compassion, and I admire tremendously the way you adjusted to this changed society without losing your integrity.'

Jill leans into me, 'Oh Mum I'm sorry about what I said. I guess I'm not being much help to you. Of course you should go if you want to, but I'll miss you and three years is a long time in the life of my children when they're so young. The other thing worrying me is that travel can be so dangerous now, with terrorist groups blowing up buildings and buses and airports. There's also been a few accidents at take-off with these new airships.'

'Well I gather you'd advise me against going,' I laugh.

Jill laughs too and says, 'I'm not going to make it too easy for you to disappear from my life for three years.'

At that moment Abdullah comes running in from the lounge room saying, 'Come and see my tower Nanna. It's nearly as tall as me.'

After I praise his building efforts we return to the kitchen for a lunch of cold meat and salad. Abdullah grizzles a bit about eating the sliced tomato, but Jill is firm with him and eventually he eats up everything on his plate. I have seen some of the young mothers letting their boy children get away with abominable behaviour, but Jill is just as strict with her son as she is with her daughters.

After lunch we have a little wander around my garden and I let Abdullah pull some baby carrots. I help him wash them, and then we pack them into a plastic container for him to take home to share with his big sisters.

Jill's chauffer/gardener arrives later in the afternoon. I wave them off and then sit for a while in the seat on the verandah. I had hoped talking to Jill would help me decide whether or not I should go with Joe and his children. Instead I feel more confused and torn. I also feel as if I have failed to show my younger and more amenable daughter how I felt, for I have certainly always loved her just as much as her more vital and rebellious sister.

During the next week I spend hours agonising over and over in my mind what I should do. I know I am of great importance in the lives of Joanna and Thomas, and that they would miss me badly if I don't go. They will be in a totally strange world and my familiar presence there would help them to settle in. I also know how much I would miss those two precious grandchildren, for I am much more closely bonded with them than with Jill's children.

I get to the stage where I have definitely decided to go, and then I think about how it would be to never see Jill again. I've had to learn to live without one of my daughters, and now I'm planning to deliberately cut the other one from my life. Wouldn't I hurt her feelings terribly by going? Wouldn't I be verifying what she already feels; that I have loved Fiona the most. In choosing to leave I would be showing that her sister's children are more important and loved more dearly by me than she and her children are.

While my love for Jill and all the grandchildren is the main cause for my indecision there are other considerations as well. I am quite fearful of what the future would hold if I went. Travelling so far could be dangerous. Terrorists of different cults and religions are a problem all around the world, and frequently target the airports for their attacks.

As well as fearing this I am nervous at the thought of flying. The relatively new airships frequently experience problems that result in forced landings and even crashes. Living in a foreign country would also be very challenging, because I would have to learn the language and cultural practices if I am to help the children adjust to their new life. Behind all these concerns is the other fear, the fear of the unknown; fear of how we would escape from Saudi Arabia and of where we would finish up if we were successful.

After a week Joe comes to ask me what my decision is, and seems quite surprised when I say I can't go.

At first he appeals to my grandmotherly love. 'You do know how important you are to Joanna and Thomas,' he says and adds, 'and you'll miss each other so much.'

I answer, 'Of course I know this. Please don't make things harder for me than it is, but if I go I wouldn't ever see Jill again or my other grandchildren.'

Joe interrupt me, 'But what about you as a person, as a woman. Surely you can't be happy living this life where there are so many restrictions and limitations. Have you thought about what your situation would be if Ali should die? Your life is totally dependent on him.'

I know that things would be easier for Joe in Saudi Arabia if I were along to help with the children, but I also know he cares about my well-being and wants me to be happy. I try to explain to him how I am torn by the different loves I feel, but also that I am fearful of the initial flight and of an unknown and unknowable future. I think he thinks less of me by the time I have explained my feelings, but he gives me a hug before leaving.

A week later we are all at the airport to see Joe and the children leave. Because of heightened security at airports all around the world, only passengers are allowed into the airport proper. Those who come to see off the travellers must to say their farewells either outside or in a long corridor that leads to the entry gates.

Jill and Ali and their four children are at the airport when I drive up with Joe and the children. I know this will be my last chance to snuggle with these two precious ones, so on the way to the airport I hold them close savouring the clean, fresh smell of their hair and their strong, little bodies pressed close to mine. As I hold them for this one last time I feel my heart is breaking; it really feels as though something fragile and glasslike is shattering inside my chest, and it will never be mended.

When we get out of the car the cousins all hug each other, and then Joanna and Thomas hug their aunt and uncle before giving me one last cuddle and kiss.

As I watch the little family walking away down the corridor I burst into tears and sob and sob. Jill holds me close, but the little girls and Abdullah just stare at me with worried eyes. They haven't seen Nanna crying before and they don't know what to make of it.

As I write these words I feel tears begin to well up in my eyes and brush them away with the back of my hand. I really must take a break.

2055 - 2060

I've had a bit of lunch and now feel strong enough to continue. This part will be easier, for there is some happiness to write about.

Within a fortnight of them leaving I receive the first letter from Joe and hand-made cards from Joanna and Thomas. Another Australian family, who are also going to Riyadh, boarded the airship in Sydney. The father, a man called Derek Smith, is going to work on the same project as Joe, and he has two children, a boy aged eleven and girl of eight. Joanna and Thomas had spent much of the journey with them playing board games in the spacious children's area. Although the trip took four days it had been very pleasant. There was comfortable seating and sleeping accommodation and excellent service. Joe had never travelled on a jet plane, but had heard of how cramped the seating had been. He felt that what had been lost in speed was more than made up for in comfort.

He also described what they saw when the airship travelled below the clouds. The captain of the airship supplied them with maps, which showed the world before and after the rise in water levels. Joe and the children poured over them noting the changes.

He reported on how strange it was to fly over the Indian Ocean, which is now devoid of any islands, and to see how the Red Sea and the waters of the Persian Gulf have infiltrated into the coastal regions of Saudi Arabia. From the air they saw that these coastal areas were lined with desalinisation plants. Joe said these plants had been imported from Australia to supply water to the farms that now dot the land.

Before leaving Joe learnt that Saudi Arabia is still a monarchy ruled by the Saud Family, but now the royal family members run the farms. Instead of following their leisurely, opulent life style of the previous oil-rich decades they now organise the work on the land and supervise the solar and desalinisations plants.

When Joe and the children eventually arrived at Riyadh they were met at the airport by the Australian envoy and driven to their new home. They have been provided with good accommodation in a compound on the outskirts of the city and the Smith family's house is next door to theirs. The children are starting school the following week, and Anne Smith has offered to mind them after school if Joe is late back from work.

It seems everything is working out well for them, and knowing the children will have a motherly person looking out for them makes me feel less guilty about not going with them.

The children's messages are brief, but they sound happy, although Joanna says she misses me and wishes I was there.

I write back straight away, being careful about what I say because Joe has warned me that all mail is now censored. Before he left he stressed to me that on no account was I to allude to his plan to defect, or to say anything critical about the regime now ruling our country.

For the next two years Joe and I correspond with both of us being careful about what is included in our letters. Joe is working hard and often has to be away from Riyadh for a few days. Evidently Anne Smith is wonderful with the children, and cares for them along with her own two in the absence of the men.

Reading between the lines I gather Joe is no more satisfied with the education and life training Joanna is receiving in Saudi Arabia than that which she had been experiencing in Australia. Because of this I know Joe's plan to defect when the opportunity arises must still be a possibility, and that I will only know about it after it has happened.

For me the bright spots in my life are when I receive Joe's letters. It had taken their absence to make me realise just how important a part of my life Joanna and Thomas were. Now time hangs heavily on my hands.

Jill is aware of how much I miss this little family and tries to include me more in the lives of her children. She sends the car a couple of times a week to collect me and take me to her house where we spend the day together. We work in her garden or swim in her pool when the weather is fine. Later in the day we walk to the girl's school, which is nearby, and accompany Sara, Amani and Fatima home. They are dear little girls, very affectionate and happy, but they seem to lack the verve and intelligence I loved so much about Joanna. I feel somehow lacking because I can't relate as closely with them as I had with her.

It is the same with Abdullah. He is now attending the top Muslim boys' school in the city and the chauffer/gardener drives him there each day and collects him each afternoon. When he was younger Jill had treated him in the same way as the girls, and he had been a good little boy. Once he turned five Ali took over his upbringing and, in my opinion, Abdullah now gets away with murder. It appears to me he is virtually allowed to do as he wishes and is treated by his father like a little tin god. The family eat together, but the girls help with the serving of the food while he sits next to his father and is waited on by his older sisters.

Unlike his sisters he has no chores that he is expected to do around the house, and I can see that this preferential treatment is having a detrimental effect on him. Although he is not quite six he is already arrogant and self-opinionated and has lost much of the charm and sweetness he'd had when younger.

Apart from spending more time with Jill and her family I try to fill the gap left by the absence of Joe and the children in other ways.

I begin going to the Women's Centre once a week and it is here that I once more catch up with both Ruth and Suzie. I also spend much more time with my neighbour Amy.

Although her husband is bedridden he doesn't want to tie her to him and the house. She leaves food and drink for him on a side table near his bed before he happily waves us off for a day of bushwalking on the mountain. These days are a joy for both of us because we feel so free of the restrictions that are now such a part of our daily lives. We can walk for miles without having to worry about being covered from head to foot and having our movements restricted by ground-dragging capes. Initially we wear old jeans, but when they wear out we don pantaloons we have made and push the surplus material down into our walking boots.

Together we explore all the walking trails on the mountain and beyond, stopping for picnic lunches on high cliffs or beneath beautiful waterfalls. These days with Amy are marvellously invigorating, and seem to both of us like a step back to the past, back to a time when we had been allowed to be active and free instead of the submissive, covered creatures society now demands that we be.

The weekly letters I receive from Joe continue to be the highlight of my week, and I read them several times before putting them away in a special box. Sometimes, when I am feeling especially lonely, I get out the box and reread the letters from the first to the latest one. In this way I feel I am sharing in the lives of Joanna and Thomas.

By the time Joe and the children have been living in Saudi Arabia for two years I have begun to think he must have given up the idea of defecting. I even begin to look forward to the time when Joe's three-year contract will be completed and they will all return home to Australia. I let myself imagine how wonderful it will be to see Joanna and Thomas again, and think about how much they will have changed.

Surprisingly mail between the two countries seems to be handled efficiently, and usually I receive Joe's letters regularly every Wednesday during these years. Occasionally one is a day or two late, but this is the exception rather than the rule. Because of this I'm not particularly concerned when, one week, no letter has arrived by the Friday.

I have just checked the mailbox and am walking back up my drive when a long, black saloon turns into my entryway. I step aside to let it pass, and then hurry up to see who these unexpected visitors are. As I draw alongside the car two officers from the Internal Security Force step briskly from the driver's and front passenger seats. They wear the midnight blue uniforms and matching peaked caps of this group, and both men are extremely tall and powerfully built.

Although I have seen members of the Security Force standing behind our leader on propaganda television programmes I have never actually seen any of them in the flesh, and they look very formidable. Unlike the members of the Militia, who are a ubiquitous presence, the members of the Security Force are not seen often in public. Their work is more secret, their powers unknown, and because of the secrecy surrounding their activities they are feared even more than the Militia.

As they approach me my heart begins to race and I feel my legs go weak. My mind is in turmoil. What are they doing here? Why am I getting a visit from members of this secret force?

Each man takes hold of me by the elbows and in a peculiar way I feel comforted by their support. While they hold me a third man alights from the back seat of the car and approaches me. He too is dressed in the midnight blue uniform of the other two, but he has gold amulets on the shoulders and gold braid trimming on his cuffs.

Holding out a card he identifies himself as Commander Mc. Fee then says, 'This is Officer Hall and Officer Jameson We have some questions for you Mrs. Harper. Perhaps you could lead us inside and we can get started.'

His manner is abrupt and unfriendly, but I am determined to hide my growing fear. I am also having difficulty coming to terms with the fact that these three members of the feared Internal Security Force are all Australians. I had for some reason always thought this force would be made up of men from other countries, but now I remember how the original armed forces had metamorphosed into the Militia and Security Force, and that new recruits were chosen from the boys' state schools. The realisation of Australian men's involvement in this feared group only adds to my fear and confusion.

I shrug off the officers controlling hands and say as calmly as I can manage, 'Come this way,' as I usher them through the front door and into the lounge room.

With pretended assurance I ask, 'How can I help you gentlemen?' but I address my query to Commander Mc. Fee.

He answers suavely, 'May we be seated? This might take some time.'

His remark makes me instantly more ill at ease, and I flush at being made to feel remiss as a hostess. After the three men are seated I make a stammering offer of tea or coffee, but he stops me mid-sentence with the cutting remark, 'This is not a social call Mrs. Harper.'

Regaining some semblance of self-control I ask, 'Why are you here?'

With a false laugh the Commander says, 'As you are no doubt aware your son-in-law has left Saudi Arabia illegally, and we have reason to believe he and his children are now somewhere in one of the countries of the United European Community. We are hoping you can help us with information as to their whereabouts.'

I am overwhelmed by a sudden savage feeling of joy that my precious little family has made it to a freer land, but this is soon followed by a lurch of fear. What lengths will the Saudis go to get them back, and what makes these men think I know anything about where they might be?

I am glad I can say quite truthfully, 'I have no idea where they might be. This is the first I've heard about them leaving Saudi Arabia, and I have absolutely no idea where they would go.'

The Commander leans forward in his chair and says softly, 'Isn't it true that you and your son-in-law have corresponded regularly during the past two year?'

'We have, but at no time has Joe even hinted at the likelihood of them leaving the country. He seemed pleased with the way the project has progressed, and the children appeared to be happy and settled.'

To convince him of my ignorance regarding the defection I add tearfully, 'This has come as a shock to me. I was looking forward to them coming back to Australia at the end of this year.'

I don't think I am convincing enough because he then says, 'Have you kept the letters you've received from your son-in-law?'

I feel like lying, but then I fear that they will search my house and find the box. If they are forced to do this it will make it look as if I have something to hide, so I nod my head.

He says, not unkindly, 'I'm afraid we will have to confiscate any letters you have so they can be analysed for clues as to where Mr. Edgerton and his children may have gone.'

I walk into the bedroom and bring out the box, but before handing it over say, 'I can assure you there is nothing in any of these that even suggests Joe planned to leave. You will find it a waste of time trying to find in them any clues as to where he and the children are.'

The Commander smirks, 'That may be so Mrs. Harper, but you would be surprised how efficient our analysts can be.'

It dawns on me that perhaps they will look for some sort of code in the letters, and I feel thankful Joe and I have never thought to do anything so devious. We have just been careful about what we mentioned because we knew our correspondence would be censored.

As the men rise to leave I say, 'I know you have to do your job, but these letters are very precious to me. Would it be possible for me to have them back after they've been analysed?'

He assures me he will see what he can do and they leave.

After their car disappears down my drive I sink down onto the old couch on the verandah and take a deep breath. I realise that all the time they have been here I have been shallow breathing, and as a consequence am feeling quite light-headed. Now I have time to take in what I've been told I think of Joe and the children. How have they escaped and where are they now? I know Joe would only do what was best for the children, and I hope so much they will be safe.

I also mull over the knowledge that there are Australian men in the feared Internal Security Force. From watching propaganda programmes on television in the past I had known about the initial reorganisation of the armed forces into the National Militia. I also knew that further recruits to this and the Internal Security Force were chosen from the state schools and trained at the Academy instead of going to one of the Vocational Colleges. Despite this knowledge I had always assumed the black shades worn by these men hid dark Arab eyes because they were such a part of the despotic rule under which we now live. I feel foolish about this misconception, but also upset at having to face the fact that Australian men are active participants in the making of this repressive society.

Commander Mc. Fee looked about sixty so he would have originally been a member of the armed forces, but the two officers are young, probably in their early twenties. I wonder what criteria are used to select the boys who will attend the Academy. Going by these two today perhaps size is a factor in their selection. Are the schoolyard bullies selected, or perhaps those boys who obey instructions blindly are more likely to be deemed suitable?

As I sit there my mind teases at this thought, but it keeps coming back to the unalterable fact; these imposers of the laws are Australians. This fact fills me with a sense of utter hopelessness.

In the following days the Commander and his officers visit Joe's parents, search their house and confiscate letters they have received from Joe.

They also check Ali's emails. He is uncomfortable about this, and I'm pretty sure he's angry with Joe for creating problems with the authorities for him and his family.

When I ask Ali about what further steps will be taken to try to find Joe and the children he answers rather crossly, 'I don't know Mother Marion. If they've managed to get to one of the countries in the United European Community they'll probably be safe. It hasn't been good for me, having a brother-in-law who has defected, so I just hope it's all forgotten as soon as possible.'

I can understand why Ali feels this way, but his answer upsets me. In some ways he is so self-centred.

During the next few months I feel utterly miserable. It is almost like losing that little family all over again. I realise how much I had been hoping they would return when Joe's contract expired, but I also know this was a very selfish wish. I know I should be happy for them.

At times I do rejoice at the thought of them living in a free society where Joanna can get a good education, and Thomas will grow up with a fair and realistic attitude towards women. There are other times though when I simply long for some word from them, a letter saying that they are safe and happy, but of course this is now impossible because the authorities could trace any mail to its source.

The silence from the other side of the world is re-sounding, and I don't even have Joe's letters to look back on because of course they are never returned to me.

I spend several weeks wondering how they are and if I will ever hear from Joe again. The hoped for letter finally comes one day when I return from the Women's Centre.

I had gone there with Amy and afterwards we visited the garden centre to buy tomato plants, so it is almost dark when we reach our bus stop and say our goodbyes at the bottom of my drive. When I push open the front door I hear a quiet rustle and looking down see a brown envelope that is caught part way under the door. I still haven't switched on the light, but in the gloom I make out my name, and my heart skips a beat as I recognise Joe's handwriting. I push the door shut and bend to pick up the letter, and then rush across the room to turn on the reading lamp above my armchair. I am so excited and emotional tears come to my eyes. It is a while before I can focus on the words.

Of course I no longer have the letter, but it was long and newsy and even all these years later I still remember most of what he wrote. Joe told of how they had escaped by travelling at night across desert tracks until they reached the Mediterranean Sea, and then made their way on a small fishing boat to Catanzaro, a small village in southern Italy.

The Smith family escaped with them, and it had been quite a scary trip as the small boat was overloaded with nine people on board and at times the sea was rough. They had settled in France and both the children were attending good schools and were already fluent in French. Joe has obtained a position in a technical laboratory where he and his colleagues were working on improved miniaturized solar panels that would revolutionise the use of this important power source.

He said the children still missed me, and that he regretted I had not chosen to come with them because he was sure that I would have had a better life in France.

The letter finished with him saying he would keep in touch from then on, and that letters would still usually be delivered on a Wednesday. He also stressed that I must destroy any mail I received from him because he feared the authorities in Australia would continue to try to trace him.

I read and reread that letter until it was committed to memory, and then I burnt it over the sink and flushed the ashes down the drain.

During the next three years I virtually live for those letters. Although I spend quite a lot of my time with my other grandchildren, I have to admit that what is happening in the lives of Joanna and Thomas continues to be more important to me. In one way I suppose that what Jill had said to me so many years ago was true. I do love my two absent grandchildren more than Sara, Amani and Fatima, and certainly more than Abdullah who is growing up to be a spoilt brat.

Shortly before my seventieth birthday I receive a momentous letter from Joe.

By this time they have been in France for nearly four years. I haven't seen him or the children for almost six years, but not a day has gone by when I haven't thought about them and missed them.

In this letter Joe says there are concerns throughout the United European Community about what is happening to women in Australia, and he and the children are worried about whether I will continue to be safe. Rumours are rife there that elderly widows are being euthanized in our country.

Anne Smiths' parents have been finding life in Australia intolerable, and she fears for her mother's safety if her father dies. Derek is arranging for them to escape from Australia and join their family in France. Joe writes that from what little information he has gathered about life in Australia things are only going to get worse, particularly for women. If I want to get out he can arrange for me to accompany Anne's parents.

Because I can't answer him he gives complete instructions about what I should do if I choose to go, and how I can contact him once I arrive in Indonesia. He finishes the letter by saying how much Joanna and Thomas miss me and that they hope I will come.

I have very little time in which to decide and my mind goes into panic mode. I really can't think clearly. As you get older it takes longer to make decisions, even little things like what you will wear that day or the sort of cheese you wish to buy. This is so much bigger.

For a long while I just sit in my armchair reading and rereading Joe's letter and his instructions on what I must do if I choose to escape from Australia and make a new life for myself in France.

During this time I think often of the wonderful time Bill and I had spent in France. After our holiday in Italy we dreamed of one day travelling again, and in 2024 we decided that if we didn't go then we never would. The wars in Iraq and Afghanistan had both ended in the ignominious retreat of the American and allied forces, and religious leaders now ruled both countries. A degree of harmony had been attained in the Middle East with Israel finally conceding the Palestinians the right to some land.

We thought it would be a reasonably safe a time to travel, although there continued to be random terrorist attacks in various parts of the world.

The other thing affecting our decision to take that long-awaited trip was that the price of petroleum products continued to rise steeply as supplies became scarcer and more expensive to source. This had resulted in a continuing increase in the cost of airfares, and we felt if we didn't go then we wouldn't be able to afford it later on.

At that time Dad was a spry and healthy seventy-nine and he happily agreed to move into our house and mind the girls. They both adored him because he spent endless time with them playing their silly games. He was also the most marvellous storyteller, and they sat entranced while he told them the myths and legends of the ancient world.

Before our holiday in Italy we had tossed up whether to go there or to France, so when the girls were old enough to be left with my father we began planning our trip to France. We both had long service leave due so added a couple of weeks of that to the school vacation. Our plan was to do a walking trip around the Dordogne Region and then spend two weeks in Paris.

It was a wonderful holiday marred only by the intense security then existing at all airports. When we landed in Singapore all the passengers were practically strip-searched, and on our arrival at De Gaulle Airport all hand luggage was opened and searched. The terrorist attacks that had begun in the early years of the twenty-first century continued unabated, and the number of proponents of these attacks increased. There seemed to be an endless number of disaffected groups who were willing to harm innocent people in order to have their voices heard.

Bill and I were booked into a rather posh hotel near the Champs-Elysees, but after all the hours of travelling, and the long time spent at the airport on landing, we simply collapsed into the comfortable bed and slept until noon the next day.

Before leaving the hotel we organised our walking packs and arranged with the hotel to store our other luggage until we returned. We caught the fast train to Souillac and from there we commenced our walking holiday, armed with a comprehensive map that showed all the walking tracks in the area and a list of hotels and chateaus in each town through which we would pass.

It was September and the weather was lovely. Each day we planned our route then bought bread, pates, cheese and fruit for our lunches. During the next two weeks we walked many kilometres, up steep hills, through leafy lanes and along the edges of high, white cliffs. The scenery was magnificent and for much of the time we could see the beautiful Dordogne River shining in the distance. One thing that impressed me greatly was the way many of the walking tracks went through the properties of small landholders. As we passed, the men and women working in their vegetable gardens and orchards or feeding their pigs or geese looked up and waved. Bill and I thought how different they were from most Australian farmers who were likely to threaten you with a dog or a gun if you walked on their land.

We stayed at several picturesque towns but there are two I remember particularly. One was Rocamadour, a spectacular town built on the side of a steep hill and a destination for many pilgrims during the Middle Ages. The other was a tiny village called Meyronne where we stayed in a very old château and enjoyed a wonderful gourmet meal seated on a balcony overlooking a tree-filled valley.

The Dordogne Region was a gourmet's delight. It was famous for foie gras and truffles, and also most vegetables and many different kinds of fruit trees flourished in the area. During those two weeks Bill and I ate like royalty. Our time there gave me an appreciation of why the French had long been seen as the gourmets of the world. All the food we ate was produced locally. Whether prepared by a chef of note in a large town or a housewife running a small pension in a tiny village, the food was always good because it was fresh.

In the world of today, transportation is slow and costs are high. Because of this most countries have had to adjust their cuisine to those products that can be locally sourced. In this the rest of the world is finally doing what the French had done for centuries.

After our two weeks of walking we returned to Paris and spent a wonderful time visiting all the galleries, shopping at the markets and eating great food in little hidden- away restaurants. We also made a couple of trips out of the city, one to visit Monet's house and garden and another to Auvers-sur-Oise where Van Gogh painted many of his finest works.

The shops were exciting and full of stylish clothes, so different from anything available in Australia. Bill was very patient while I shopped for clothes and bags and shoes for myself, as well as dresses for Fiona and Jill.

Since that holiday, France had always held a special place in my memory. How foolish I would be not to return there now that I have the chance.

The instructions from Joe are very precise. I would have to be at Crescent Bay at exactly six a.m. on a specified date. There I would be taken by dingy to a boat that would be moored in the bay. This boat would take me to Eden, where I would transfer onto a deep-sea fishing boat, and meet up with Anne's parents and another couple who were also escaping to join their family in Italy. We would travel on this fishing boat to Indonesia and from there we could catch an airship to France.

The irony of escaping by this route is not lost on me because I well remember the refugees from war-torn lands who risked their lives as they made the hazardous trip via Indonesia in leaky boats during the early years of the twenty-first century. We saw these people on television as their old and fragile boats were being towed ashore by coast guards. They always looked half-starved, ragged and desperate as they were herded onto buses to be taken to the infamous detention camps for processing. If I went I would become a boat person in reverse.

Thinking about those desperate boat people I wonder if I am desperate enough, or indeed brave enough, to do as they had done.

I have a week to make my decision, and I must admit I am very tempted. I can't help wishing I had gone five years earlier with Joe and the children when I could have made the trip in relative safety. To go now would be much more hazardous and I am that much older, but now life in Australia has become much more regimented. Five years ago the restrictions had only just begun. Now the years of financial dependency, of surveillance, of being a second-class citizen have taken a toll on me; have hardened my discontent. So often I feel isolated, lonely and angry.

During these years I have continued to miss Joanna and Thomas even more than I had thought I would. So often I have wished I were there with them, seeing them growing up and being a part of the new and interesting things they are experiencing in France. Compared with them Jill's girls are living boring, unstimulating lives. Frequently my love for them is tinged with regrets and sometimes anger at how accepting they are.

During the week I have in which to make my decision I vacillate as I had five years earlier.

Some days I think that of course I will go; leave behind this life of appalling restrictions, and change it for one where I could go where I wished and wear what I chose. Most importantly I would be able to once more see my beloved grandchildren daily.

Other days I think of the negatives. The journey itself would be quite dangerous, and even if I arrive safely I will be a financial burden on Joe unless I can get a job of some sort. The other thing bothering me is how Joanna and Thomas will be with me now they are teenagers. Will they still feel that special bond we'd had, or will they see me as an irrelevance in their present lives?

On the night before I am to leave I still haven't made up my mind, but I pack a small canvas bag. I put in the few clothes I think will be suitable to wear on a small boat and some precious personal possessions, including the photograph of Bill I keep on my bedside table and a couple of Jill and her children.

I do intend to go. I have worked out it will probably take me an hour and a half to walk there, and set my alarm clock for four thirty before lying down to rest. During the night I doze intermittently, but then I wake and lie staring into the dark worrying about what lies ahead for me.

When the alarm goes off I dress in my warmest clothes and comfortable shoes and put on the backpack. I know I will have to wear my cape, but when I try to get it on over the backpack it sticks out behind, making me feel and look like a hunchback.

I remember an old story my grandfather used to tell me about the Hunchback of Notre Dame. Although I had found the thought of this creature frightening I still loved to hear the story.

I don't think the sight of me as a brown caped hunchback would strike fear in the hearts of anyone, but I would draw attention to myself. Even at this early hour of the morning there could be militiamen patrolling the streets of the city that I must pass through to get to the river.

I throw off the cape and stand in my doorway, looking down the dark driveway and then off to the lights of the city in the distance. I imagine myself unencumbered by that restricting garment striding fearlessly through the darkness until I reach the bay, where I will step lightly into the dinghy that will take me to the waiting boat. I imagine boarding this boat to freedom. I think of how exciting it will be travelling across the world in an airship, and finally landing in a country where the women lead normal, productive lives, and where I will see my beloved grandchildren again.

I kick the cape aside, step down from the verandah and stride down my driveway to the road. Then I stop. I can go no further. Fear of what I might encounter overwhelms me. I begin to shake and tears stream down my face. I know I can't go. I have become too cowardly, too fearful and too old.

2060 -2070

For the first few weeks after I failed to take the opportunity to escape Joe had organised for me I don't receive a letter. I feel frustrated because there is no way I can explain to Joe and the children my reasons for not going. During these weeks I also fret about my cowardice, and often wish I'd had the courage to go.

When a letter finally arrives it is from Joanna, and since then she has been my main correspondent, with the occasional note included from Joe and Thomas.

At the time I thought Joe stopped writing because he was angry with me for not coming after he had spent time and undoubtedly a considerable amount of money trying to help me. This made me sad because we had been close, but there was no way of explaining to him how fearful and cowardly I had become from living under this repressive regime.

In one of her letters Joanna tells me she took over writing to me because Joe had begun a serious relationship with a French woman called Monique. Evidently he felt it would be strange to continue writing to the mother of his first wife once he had another woman in his life. This is the reason he gave Joanna for handing over this task to her but I can't help feeling he was probably more than a little peeved with me for being such a coward.

Throughout the years Joanna continues to write regularly and from her letters I am kept up to date with what is happening in the lives of this much loved trio. I know when first Joanna and then Thomas gain their degrees and when she starts working. She writes me a long, newsy letter after her skiing trip in Switzerland with friends from the university and another about her travels through several European countries by train. She goes on this trip with Pierre, and from this letter I gain the distinct impression that this young man is more important than others she has told me about.

Joanna's letters give me a window into what is happening in another part of the world, a glimpse into a world we Australian women have lost, one where women still have choices and the opportunity to lead useful, active and fulfilling lives.

Sara and her sisters are leading such narrow and boring lives by comparison. There is only a year's difference between Joanna and Sara, but when Joanna was beginning at university with a world of knowledge and new experiences opening before her Sara had finished all the schooling she would get. Her life since then involved helping Jill around the house until she married and moved to a house of her own.

Often when I spent time with my granddaughters during their teenage years I felt impatient with their lack of curiosity and the limitations of their interests. I tried to stimulate them by talking about events from the past or novels I had enjoyed or artists who I admired. They listened politely, but I'm sure they felt I was being an old bore. They really only seemed interested in clothes, makeup, silly romance novels and of course boys. At times, when they giggled away together about some young man who had come to dinner with his parents, I'd think impatiently how empty-headed they were.

I'm being a little unfair to Amani with these criticisms. She seems to have a more enquiring mind than her older and younger sisters. When she was quite young she demonstrated a talent for painting and produced some stunning works of flowers and fruit. She listened intently when I described to her the paintings of enormous flowers Georgia O'Keefe had produced way back in the earlier part of the twentieth century, and when I told her about our own Margaret Olley whose still life paintings of flowers and fruit made her one of the most successful and admired artists in Australia.

As a teenager Amani also seemed to want to do more than her sisters. She wasn't content to sit around the house reading or sewing as they were. Instead she worked in the garden with Jill and also taught painting at the girls' school two days a week.

By the time Sara turns eighteen she is married to a man chosen for her by Ali and the following year is expecting her first child. This is also the year Amani gets engaged to Jim. He is the son of one of Ali's work colleagues and they met at a large party that had been organised for departmental employees and their families. There was an instant attraction between the young couple, and they were both happy when their fathers arranged that they should wed.

It is around the time of Amani's engagement that I have the contact with my granddaughters curtailed.

I had recently received a letter from Joanna in which she wrote about the trip she'd taken during the university vacation. She is beginning the final year of her degree, and wrote enthusiastically about the subjects she will be studying in the coming year. I guess it is the comparison between her life and those of my other granddaughters that leads me to speak out more than I should.

On this particular day the chauffer collects me quite early, and when I arrive at the house Jill and the three girls are sitting in the lounge room planning the engagement party. They are making a list of who will be invited and are discussing what food should be served. When I walk into the room they all greet me with hugs and kisses and make room for me on the big, semi-circular couch. At this time Sara is nineteen, Amani seventeen and Fatima fifteen, three lovely young woman.

Amani asks, 'What do you think Nanna? Should we just serve finger food or do you think we should have a sit down dinner?'

As I don't even know how many people will be attending this party I answer, 'It depends on the number of people you're inviting, but personally I like the idea of serving finger food or having a buffet. It's less formal and gives people a chance to mingle, which is what you want at an engagement party.'

I would have thought it would be a simple decision, but we spend the rest of the morning discussing the pros and cons of the different sorts of catering and what should be served. I become bored with the conversation, so excuse myself and go for a wander in Jill's lovely gardens.

While I walk I think about my granddaughters, of Joanna and the exciting, interesting life she is leading on the other side of the world, and of Sara, pregnant at nineteen, Amani engaged at seventeen and soon to marry and Fatima, who at fifteen has finished school and will spend the next couple of years marking time until she too marries.

When I return to the house the lists have finally been put aside. Sara is sitting at the dining room table while Jill and the other two girls flitter around putting out plates and cutlery and food. I sit down next to Sara and ask how she is feeling, and she answers rather dolefully that she's sick of being so lumbering and out of shape, and will be glad when the baby is born.

The others join us at the table and once more the talk is all about the impending party. Evidently one of the families to be invited includes a man who Ali thinks would be a suitable husband for Fatima although I notice that she doesn't look terribly enthusiastic about this possible suitor.

Jill says, rather reflectively, 'I don't suppose it will be long before you're engaged too.'

I feel cross with my daughter's acceptance of what is happening to her daughters and say 'For goodness sake, she's barely left the school room and you're already thinking about marrying her off.'

Jill looks hurt and answers, 'That's not fair Mum. You know I have very little say in it. I think Fatima should still be at school and that Amani is too young to be getting married, but Ali makes the decisions. He decided when Fatima should leave school and he approved the match between Amani and Jim.'

It is then that I let fly and say the things I will later have cause to regret.

I shout angrily, 'And you have stood back and let your girls become uneducated, submissive creatures with no ambition but to marry and have children. Have you forgotten what life used to be like for women? When we could wear what we chose, drive around the country if we so wished, work at a job that was stimulating and rewarding, earn our own money and determine how we spent it and, most importantly, choose when and whom we married.'

Jill sits silent in the face of my verbal onslaught and I uncaringly continue, 'Look at your daughters. They have no freedom to choose. They spend their days on time-filling domestic chores or endless planning, and their heads are full of romantic nonsense from the rubbish they read. They will never know what it is like to be responsible for themselves, to earn a living and have an equal relationship with a man.'

I am so carried away with what I am saying I am unaware that Ali has entered the room until he says, 'Mother Marion, I would prefer that you stop talking in this way in my home. I do not want my wife subjected to your verbal abuse, or my daughters hearing your jaundiced views. I will get the chauffer to take you home.'

So saying he leaves the room and not a word is spoken as I gather up my coat and handbag and go outside to wait for the car to be brought around.

I know I have been unduly harsh towards Jill, and that there has been little she could have done to change the course of her daughters' lives. Nevertheless I am unrepentant about what I have said. I am so full of anger from thinking about the contrast between the lives of Joanna and her cousins that I spoke out from the sense of injustice that has been building up within me for many years.

After the driver lets me out at the top of my drive I sit for a while on the verandah gradually regaining my sense of equilibrium. When I left Jill's house I had been furious about being spoken to in that way by Ali, but now I ponder the possible ramifications of him overhearing my tirade.

I am still sitting on the verandah when I hear the phone ring. I hurriedly unlock my door and race to answer it.

It's Jill sounding very upset saying, 'Mum, Ali has said that you won't be able to come to our house and see the girls if you ever talk that way again. Will you promise not to?'

I feel badly about upsetting Jill and say, 'I'm sorry he heard what I was saying.' I add, rather sarcastically, 'I might've known it would bother him.'

Then Jill surprises me, 'As a matter of fact it bothers me as well. I don't want my girls hearing about the different kind of life you and I experienced. I want them to be satisfied and happy with what they've got.'

I begin to object but Jill interjects, 'Look Mum I saw what happened to you when you tried to fight the Education Department. You finished up so obsessive and depressed I feared for your sanity. And look what happened to Fiona and some of her friends because they tried to draw attention to what was happening to women in our society. I know you might think I've taken the coward's way, but I want my daughters alive, and if they don't have the opportunities and freedoms we had so be it. All I can do is ensure they marry men who will treat them with kindness.'

After hearing this I feel regretful about my earlier attack on this gentle daughter of mine, so I say I was sorry for causing such an upset and promise to keep a tighter rein on my tongue in the future.

I find this very difficult for the next time I visit Fatima isn't there to greet me and I am told she has been confined to her room. When I ask why, Jill looks self -conscious and says she is being punished by Ali. She obviously doesn't want to talk about it so I don't question her further, but later when Amani and I are alone in the garden I ask her what Fatima has done to warrant this treatment.

Amani looks upset then says in a torrent of words, 'Oh Nanna, it was awful. The man Father has chosen for Fatima is horrible and nearly thirty but he's wealthy and has an important position in the government. After the party Father went off at Fatima for not being more friendly towards this man and she said she's in love with Joel, the gardener's son, and that she wants to marry him when they are old enough. Well Father was furious and gave her the third degree about her involvement with Joel. When she admitted that they had been meeting in the garden and had kissed, Father was furious. He even threatened to send her away to the Correctional Centre but Sara and I pleaded with him not to do that; said he couldn't possibly let our sister become a sex toy for Militia men. I think he was surprised we knew what happened to girls who displeased their father's and he doesn't usually take much notice of anything we say but he softened a bit. He said the alternative would be that she'd have her head shaved and be isolated for six months. Surprisingly Mum intervened. It's the only time I've seen Mum stand up to him. She said he was being too harsh so instead of having her head shaved Mum cut it quite short and Fatima's being kept in her room. I don't know how long she'll be kept there but Sara and I aren't even allowed to talk to her and I heard Father tell Mum that if Fatima doesn't behave herself the Correctional Centre is still an option.'

Aghast I say, 'He wouldn't do that surely?'

Amani shakes her head and shrugs her shoulders. 'I don't know. He's terribly angry with her, not only because she's refusing to have anything to do with that old man but because she'd been seeing Joel in secret.'

Later I try to talk to Jill about it but she simply says that it is Ali's right to chastise their daughter.

Because of what happened the previous week I make a valiant attempt to keep my anger under control but can't help saying, 'I can't believe you can let Fatima be treated in this way. Don't you care about the happiness of your daughter?'

Unfortunately as I am saying this Ali appears in the doorway and he looks furious.

He advances into the room and for a brief moment I think he is going to hit me. Instead he says, 'Once more you are trying to cause trouble in my household. If you cannot learn to keep your rebellious thoughts to yourself you will no longer be welcome in my home'.

Since then I have only been allowed weekly visits but perhaps my words gave Jill the impetus to intercede on Fatima's behalf. After four weeks she was allowed to leave her room but she was still banned from having anything to do with Joel. The following year another suitor was found for her who she found more to her liking than the previous older man and she married when she turned seventeen. If she still dreams of what a life with Joel would have been like I do not know. Outwardly she seems content with her husband and the life she has made with him but women now keep their true feelings hidden.

Not long after this lessening of contact with Jill and her girls I lose my beloved neighbour Amy. Her husband, who had been bed-ridden for years, dies and she barely has time to bury him before she receives a letter. She comes to me in tears, her hands shaking and a look of concern on her face. The letter informs her that she is to be rehoused at a place called Seaside Gardens. The letter is accompanied by a colourful brochure showing groups of women walking among flower-filled gardens, playing card games and sharing meals in a luxurious dining-room. She is told to pack her personal effects and be ready to move by the next day.

She cries on my shoulder, 'But I don't want to go. I don't want to leave my home. Do you think Ali could pull strings for me so that I can stay in my own place?'

I ring Ali straight away but am unable to talk to him, so I promise Amy I will ring him at home that evening. We have a cup of tea together. Before she leaves to go home I reassure her that I will do my best to get Ali to intervene on her behalf.

That night I ring him and explain the situation but he simply says, 'There's nothing I can do for your friend. It wasn't easy to get dispensation for you to remain in your home. I certainly wouldn't be able to get it for your friend.'

I answer rather shortly, 'Couldn't you at least try?'

He replies coldly, 'It would be a waste of time. Now I must hang up. I have not yet finished my dinner.'

Fuming I slam down the phone. He is a good husband to Jill and he's certainly looked out for me since Bill died, but he can be very cool and arrogant at times.

That night I lie in bed thinking about Amy. I know there is still a serious housing shortage, and that is why widows are removed from their homes, but perhaps they would let her move in with me. I decide to talk to Amy about this in the morning.

The next day I wake reasonably early and am dressing when I happen to glance out the window. There is a long black car in Amy's driveway and as I watch two men escort her out of her house, push her roughly into the back seat and drive away. She looks briefly towards my house and I feel as though she is silently hoping I can help her. I can see she is crying.

Upset about the way my friend is being treated I once more ring Ali. I tell him of my plan, and ask him to find out for me where Amy has been taken. I will never forget his answer.

In a chilling voice he says, 'She will have been taken to the Disposal Centre. The state will take care of your friend. You had best forget her Mother Marion.'

From his answer I know the rumours I had heard are true and that my dear friend will be euthanized. I feel appalled but totally helpless to do anything to save my friend.

Whether the places like Seaside Gardens and the others I had seen on television so long ago actually exist I don't know. Perhaps some mothers of the wealthy and privileged end there days in nice places like these, but there is no way I can find out about this.

Within a week a new family moves in next door. There are two boy children who play noisily in the garden, and a father I see leaving for work each weekday morning. He takes the boys to school and they catch the bus home.

I rarely see the woman. Sometimes I catch a glimpse of a brown-clad figure hanging clothes on the line, or standing at the door to greet her sons as they dawdle up their steep drive. At times I try to catch her eye hoping to start a conversation, but she never looks my way. Over the years I have never seen her leave the house and we have never spoken.

2070

This week I have spent hours at the computer reliving my long and varied life and at the same time I hope producing an accurate record of the ways in which life in Australia changed for everyone, but particularly for women during my lifetime.

Initially I thought I had plenty of time to mull over this task and write it at a more leisurely pace but things have happened that have given me a sense of urgency to get it completed. Because of recent events I also decided to complete my journal by recording a day by day entry of this past week. I do this to show how quickly a life can change when one is dependent and vulnerable.

Thursday

This was the day of my eightieth birthday and to celebrate this momentous occasion I was required to attend the hospital for a complete physical check-up. I knew I wasn't being singled out in this regard as it is now compulsory for all people over seventy to participate in this ritual.

We are told these check-ups are in our own interest, aimed at diagnosing potential medical problems. Rumour has it that they can often lead to couples being transferred to homes because of diagnosed health problems of one in the partnership. Each year at this time I feel vulnerable, but I am actually confident there is nothing wrong with me.

My appointment was for nine-thirty, but I needed to catch the eight o'clock bus to be there in time. I travelled past the stop where I usually get off to go to the Women's Centre and into the central part of the city.

In the early thirties all the old buildings in the city centre were demolished and replaced with high, white block-like buildings with walls of solar windows. These buildings were said to be the most advanced in the world in ecological sustainability. All waste generated within the buildings is treated and recycled and water is collected in large underground tanks and filtered for reuse. The solar windows produce surplus power that is fed into the national grid. All this sounds very practical, but I still miss the old sandstone buildings and the other architectural mix that once was a part of the streetscape in this area.

There are no shops in this part of town. These buildings are the administration centres for the various government bodies, and one of them is the hospital and medical centre.

I only ever come to this part of town for these annual check-ups, or to visit my granddaughters when they have babies.

As I stood before the high glass entry door, waiting for it to open I felt nervous, but told myself to calm down. I know I am extremely fit for my age, and the actual check-ups are performed efficiently and painlessly.

As soon as I handed over my form at the reception desk a man in green scrubs approached and said, 'Ah Mrs. Harper. Come this way.'

He led me into a small room, motioned for me to remove my cape then turned abruptly and left the room. As I was standing wondering where I should put my cloak a young woman entered the room. She took the garment from my hands, motioned for me to sit in the large chair in the centre of the room. First she took some blood samples then proceeded to attach wires to my forehead, wrists and ankles. I made some silly joke about being wired for sound, but she silently completed her work and left after saying, 'This will only take ten minutes. Please keep still all the time.'

In past years I had tried to make small talk with the girls who perform this task. I was curious about them because so few women now work. None of them had been willing to say anything other than give the basic instructions. I wondered how it was that they were allowed to work, or indeed had the necessary skills to perform what is probably a simple task. As none of them would enter into a conversation I was unable to find out about this. I have been left to assume they must be young women who, for whatever reason, were without a male relative who was willing to keep them, so were given gainful employment.

I am used to this procedure and did as I had been told, although it is hard to stay completely still for ten minutes. I know the wires are connected to a computer, and that somehow the wiring enables it to monitor all my physical details including blood pressure and heart rate, as well as determining if any areas of my body are not functioning correctly.

When the ten minutes was up the young woman returned to the room, detached the wires and handed me my cloak saying, 'Wait in the reception room until your name is called.'

After a short wait a message came over an invisible speaker, 'Mrs. Harper to room five please.'

I walked along a white corridor until I found the correct door. I entered a room lit by a wall of glass. The wall opposite contained banks of computers and in the centre of the room is a large black desk behind which sat a small elderly Chinese man. He motioned me to take a seat in the chair opposite the desk then shuffled some printout while I waited.

Eventually he peered short-sightedly at me over round glasses and said in a deep, guttural voice, 'You have done well. Few women live as long as you have.'

Knowing what happened to Amy and with the worry about Ruth uppermost in my mind I thought cynically to myself, 'With good reason.'

Aloud I said humbly, 'Yes. I have been lucky.'

With a gentle smile he dismissed me with, 'That will be all for now. Perhaps we will see you next year.'

Although he was smiling I felt a chill pass through my body for he seemed to emphasise the word, 'Perhaps.' I couldn't wait to get out of that cold, efficient building and into the sunshine again.

The whole procedure had taken less than half an hour. The next bus wouldn't be along for a while so I decided to stroll around the waterfront.

It has changed so much since I was young. Then the docks were full of fishing boats, many of which looked old and weather-beaten, with decks crammed with craypots and long coiled nets. These boats disappeared once the wild fish stocks became depleted because of overfishing. Now most fish are farmed on land or in pens in the rivers.

The only boats in the harbour now are luxurious, streamlined solar powered ones owned by the wealthiest men in the city, and a couple of solar fishing boats used to catch the few remaining deep sea tuna.

I walked further around the wharfs and saw what has become a rare sight, a container ship from another country. I tried to decipher its port of origin but was unable to. They were unloading big orange containers and I wondered what they might hold, for Australia has been forced to become largely self-sufficient many years ago.

I know so little about who our current trading partners are now, but I know we still get some products from a few other countries. Occasionally I see container ships from other lands moored in the docks. These are now a rare sight, and I don't know where they come from.

The huge diesel-powered container ships, which once plied the waterways of the world, have become a thing of the past. Large wind-driven ships replaced them, but they are slow and their travel times can be erratic. Because of these inefficiencies most countries have been forced to become self-sufficient, particularly as far as perishables are concerned.

I found the thoughts of the wider world and its problems confusing, so turned my mind back to reminiscing about my first car that indeed did come from Japan. I was thinking of that dear little yellow Toyota Corolla that was my first car when I heard a shout and an angry-looking man was standing on the ship and waving me away.

Fearful that I may get into trouble for being in the wrong place I scuttled back along the wharf and returned to the depot where I waited for my bus.

When I got home I had a quick snack before turning on my computer and continuing with my journal. The doctor's remark about perhaps seeing me next year had rather spooked me and I wanted to get down all that I remembered.

Friday

This day I mooched around the house feeling lonely and unsettled. Uppermost in my mind was the worry about what would probably happen to Ruth if Gerry dies. As I had no means of contacting her I knew I would have to wait until Wednesday to find out.

To take my mind off my worries I decided to make out my shopping list. It's quite a hassle having to think of everything I might need for the next week. In the past you used to be able to walk to the local shop if you ran out of milk or bread or whatever, but now those shops have all disappeared. All foodstuffs are stored in huge warehouses and ordering is computerised.

I checked my pantry cupboard, and thought what a paltry affair it was compared with my grandmother's. I noted that I needed more bread flour, sugar and tea. I saw that I also should buy new bottles of soy and tomato sauce because both were getting low. I checked the refrigerator and wrote down chicken, mince, milk and butter on my list, then went to the bathroom to make sure there was enough soap and shampoo to last for a week. I knew I have plenty of greens in my garden, potatoes and carrots stored under the house and enough onion plaits to last several months. I was all right for vegetables except for having used up my small crop of garlic so added that to my list. It seemed a very small order, but I couldn't think of anything else I might need.

With my list completed I carefully placed it where I could read it easily. I switched on the computer and when it came on I keyed in my password. The message came on the screen welcoming me to New Ways Shopping.

This is no longer a new way to shop, but the name has remained the same since its inception more than three decades ago. I waited until I got the message to commence inputting my requirements then typed them in carefully from my list. I had almost finished when I realised I hadn't included any fruit so hastily added apples and grapes to my order. There is a time allowance of one minute in which to check the list then it disappears from the screen and a message comes up saying "Processing". After this a total of the cost comes up and a message saying "Insert Your Pin Number." When you insert this number there is a short wait followed by the message, "Transaction Completed." You must wait until this message disappears from the screen and then you shut down your computer.

When Bill was still alive we always received a full statement of our account following any computer transaction, but I lost this facility following the visit from the Friends.

After I completed this task I realised I've forgotten to put down cheese and I only have a small piece left. I felt really cross with myself, but knew there was nothing I could do for it would make me appear forgetful if I were to re-enter the screen for one item. This rankled with me and added to my general feeling of disquiet

Saturday

For many years now I have spent Saturdays with Jill, my granddaughters and their children. There was a time when I spent more time at Jill's house, but as mentioned earlier these visits were curtailed following my outbursts when the girls were in their teens.

I knew Jill and her daughters planned to give me a little birthday party so put on one of my better dresses, covered it with the cloak, and then sat on the verandah waiting for my lift. My mind went back to my visit to the Medical Centre and the doctor's comments. What had he meant when he'd said, 'Perhaps we will see you next year?' Even though he had spoken in a friendly way his words had sounded somewhat ominous and he seemed to emphasise the word "perhaps."

I felt anxious and the easy tears of an old woman filled my eyes. Through the film I saw Abdullah's silent, silver car speeding up the drive. I quickly wiped away my tears as his car came to a sudden stop, spraying gravel onto my flowerbeds. He is a thoughtless boy.

He stepped out of his car. 'Happy birthday Nan,' he called and then added rather abruptly, 'I'm glad you're ready to go.'

He did at least have the decency to help me down the steps, and tucked a warm rug around me as I settled into the back seat of the car. We didn't talk during the drive because a jangle of music filled the car making conversation impossible.

When we arrived at the house Abdullah helped me from the car and we walked up the path to the door. It was opened as soon as we reached it and the slender arms of Jewaher and Nara enveloped me. Hamud stood back while

I kissed the little girls and watched with his solemn dark eyes, but he allowed me to give him a hug before running off shouting, 'Grand Nan is here.'

Ali passed me in the passage with a brief greeting, 'Happy birthday Mother Marion; must rush or we'll miss the start of the game.'

He joined Abdullah in the car and they careened off down the street. They were going to watch a soccer match, and the haste with which they left made me feel I had been a nuisance for having to be picked up and perhaps making them late.

The little girls held my hands as we entered the lounge room and Jill came towards me with a welcoming hug and kiss. As I held her I thought how frail and small she felt through her long, cotton gown. At nearly fifty she still has the body of a young girl. It is hard to believe she has borne four children and is now the grandmother of the six lively toddlers and children who seemed to fill up the room. I bent to hug Musab and Faisal, but they were engrossed in a building project and accepted my kisses nonchalantly while continuing their game. Baby Josseph walked towards me on his short, plump legs and I picked him up and hugged him close. He is an adorable little boy with his mother's blonde curls and his father's dark eyes, a stunning combination.

I said to him, 'You get bigger every week,' and Fatima laughingly said, 'It's no wonder, the amount he eats.'

As she said this Sara and Amani appeared from the kitchen carrying large trays laden with sandwiches and little pastries. They placed the food on the long, low coffee table that dominated the centre of the room. Unlike Fatima these two granddaughters have dark, straight hair that streamed down their backs as they leant forward with the trays. They are both tall and looked graceful in the floor length shifts all the young women now wear. As they hugged me I felt the soft rolls of fat around their waists; the result of the inactive lives they lead. Holding Amani I also felt the small bump in her stomach, for she is four months pregnant with her third child.

These young women have been bought up in a segregated world where sports like net ball, hockey and tennis isn't taught in the schools and strenuous physical activity is not encouraged. Jill is slimmer and fitter than any of her daughters because she swims regularly in the lap pool Ali put in for her when the public swimming pools were closed to women. As well she still insists on doing much of her own gardening, although she has a man who comes in to do the heavy work.

Once the children had been settled on cushions around the table and were eating Jill poured tea for us and we had a brief chance to talk of adult things. Sara told me that now that Jewaher is six she has started school and loves it. I know she expected me to be pleased with this news, but I found it difficult to show sufficient enthusiasm. I know how limited the education will be that this little girl will receive.

Amani asked what I have growing at present in my vegetable garden, and we discussed the advantages of saving your own seeds for future plantings. Like her mother she is interested in gardens, but she supervises the work of others rather than actually doing any of it herself.

Fatima is expecting her second child very soon and we all talked about the baby shower Jill was planning for next Saturday.

After everyone finished eating, the spills were wiped up and the crumbs removed, then Jewaher organized the little ones into a game of schools with her being a very kind and motherly teacher. Nara and the little boys hung on her every word.

Sara said fondly, 'She's such a little mother,' and the others laughed at her pretending to be so grown up. I felt a moment of distress at the thought that being a wife and mother is all she can actually hope for, and probably this will be her fate in a few short years. It has become quite common for girls as young as fourteen or fifteen to marry. To me the lives of women are now so stunted and their choices so limited, but I am not allowed to voice these opinions.

The afternoon passed in a buzz of sweet domesticity. Too soon the men returned from their afternoon at the soccer, and the house filled with their noisy male presence. Jill's sons-in-law had been at the soccer match with Ali and Abdullah and they each hugged their children as soon as they entered the room. One very endearing quality these young men share is their strong affection for their children.

I was going to write these young Arab men but Amani's husband Jim is of old Australian parentage. He has been brought up in our New Australia though, and shares the beliefs and behaviour patterns of his brothers-in-law. All the men of his generation have grown up in households where their mothers have been dependent on and subservient to their fathers. It is natural for them to expect their wives to be the same.

The women scattered like a flock of hens as they gathered up children and toys and said hurried goodbyes. Their husbands hadn't spoken to them. They don't need to, for the women know they must be ready when their men wish to leave. At times it bothers me how little affection there seems to be between these husbands and wives, and the women seem to be so fearful of not pleasing their men. I suppose this is just part of the new way. Considering the number of children being born there must still be plenty of bonding taking place in the privacy of the bedrooms.

I too obeyed the unwritten law that a woman doesn't keep a man waiting and stood silently with my cloak pulled around me and waited patiently for Abdullah to be ready to take me home.

Once more we made the trip accompanied by the loud jangling music he seems to love. I was so pleased when the journey ended, and I was once more in the warmth and solitude of my home. I'm also pleased Abdullah doesn't bother to escort me from the car. Sometimes, usually on a Wednesday but sometimes on a Saturday, there is a letter from Joanna pushed under the door. I would be in serious trouble if he or anyone else were to see it. I have never known who delivers these precious letters, or by what circuitous route they make their way to my door, but through the years they have brought me great joy.

Today there was still no letter from Joanna and I felt a little rush of disappointment. I hoped there would be one next Wednesday, for it is a while since I have heard from her.

I removed my heavy outer garments and put on the kettle for a cup of tea. While it boiled I made a cheese sandwich and turned on the television. The girls had told me there was a good programme on at seven, something they called a domestic drama, and I was curious to see what they considered to be good.

I settled myself in my favourite chair with my tea and sandwich as the opening credits rolled. I would like to be able to say that I was soon engrossed in the story but I can't. To me it was absolute rubbish, and reminded me of the sitcoms so popular at the end of the twentieth century. The only difference was that some of those had shown men behaving foolishly. In this the man was depicted as sensible and organised in the face of his wife's decidedly frivolous and sometimes foolhardy behaviour.

After watching the programme for ten minutes I couldn't stand it a moment longer so switched off the set. I felt disappointed with my granddaughters for enjoying such crass entertainment. Then I thought of the way in which they have been educated, and the influences that are around them all the time, and I just felt sad for them.

I couldn't help wondering if Jill also watches and enjoys this woeful form of entertainment. She has changed so much that at times I simply cannot see any trace of the free, fun-loving little girl she was growing up. Mind you she was never quite as adventurous as her sister Fiona.

Without the noisy banter from the television set my house suddenly felt unnaturally quiet so I touched the remote for music and selected the classics programme. The music built to a crescendo and then gently faded away. In the ensuing silence I heard the wind building up outside and rattling a loose piece of iron on the roof of my house. I wondered if I dared climb the ladder to fix it. I know this would be foolhardy but I hate asking Ali for help. I must appear able to cope alone.

The Vivaldi had been very beautiful and calming so I decided to replay it while I wrote a further entry in my journal. As the music relaxed me I thought how good it is that there has never been any attempt made to censor classical music. Perhaps there are enough men of power who enjoy this music to keep it safe. I hope so.

Sunday

For a while the sun shone weakly through gathering storm clouds so I ate a quick breakfast before putting on pantaloons, a warm sweater, long socks and my cracked and worn boots. I wanted to get the plants I'd bought on Wednesday in the ground and also plant broad bean seeds.

I had already prepared the soil so it didn't take me long, which was just as well because rain started pelting down as I was putting my tools away. I was soaked by the time I made it to the back door so I showered and put on a sweater and long warm skirt.

I spent the rest of the day living in the past while I wrote my journal but by late afternoon my eyes were tired from staring at the screen and I was hungry for I hadn't eaten since breakfast. I made a sandwich and cup of tea and went to the little room we used to call the library. From there I could see the mountain, and I felt the need to gaze into distant space after staring at a screen for so long. The early rain had turned to sleet that slashed loudly on the window and concealed the view.

I rarely visit this room anymore, because it brings back such sad memories of Bill's death and the subsequent ghastly visit from the Friends.

We had loved this room. It is small and cosy and faces the mountain so captures the late afternoon sun. Together we built the shelving that covers one wall and spent many happy hours organising our books.

Influenced by Fiona, who was by then a librarian, we shelved the non-fiction books by subject and the fiction alphabetically by author. My collection of novels and English textbooks took up one large section, as did my father's history books. Bill's collection of maths and science books was smaller and he joked about this. Most of his books were from his university days and the rest related to his work, as did my father's. Mine was a more eclectic collection, and continued to grow as I found new authors to read and love.

Besides the fiction and textbooks we had one section that housed our recreational reading. Here we shelved our shared gardening and cooking books as well as ones about the native flora and fauna. My books on painting and artists were also in this section.

I'd also kept a small number of children's books; some dog-eared and tattered, but ones that had been Fiona and Jill's favourites. My secret hope had been that I would share them with grandchildren sometime in the future.

I cast my eyes over the sorry little collection that I still have and pulled from the shelves my ancient copy of Jane Eyre. Initially I was surprised at being allowed to keep this novel because a woman had written it. I suppose it was considered "safe" because, despite the heroine's sterling qualities, she was basically subservient.

I settled myself into the old chintz-covered chair facing the mountain that was swathed by a curtain of cloud. There was a sprinkling of snow at the pinnacle, and the chill in the air hinted at more to follow. I had intended to reread the old novel, but being in this room with its almost empty shelving pulled my mind back to the past and events I have tried to forget.

I sat there, the book open before me, but did not read. I thought of how Bill and I had spent happy days there either reading our separate novels or searching together through a book in order to identify a new plant or fungi we had found on the mountain, or choosing new plants we would like for the garden.

These were the happy memories, but others are so sad. It was in this room that Bill died and where, only a week later, I'd had to face the realisation of how totally my life would be changed with him gone.

I tried once again to read the book in my lap. At the time of the visit from the Friends I had felt glad I was allowed to keep it, but now the text seemed old fashioned although the characters and their attitudes are strangely more believable. I suppose it is natural for one's tastes and opinions to change over time, but I think the social changes I have witnessed and experienced in the past decades now makes that society more realistic. A weak sun came through the window, and the combination of its warmth and the boring book had a soporific effect on me. I curled up my legs and snoozed in the chair like an old and weary cat.

When I woke up I once more returned to my computer and wrote a further entry in my journal. There was so much to record and I felt an increasing urgency to get it all down.

Monday

As soon as I finished my breakfast I settled myself at the computer once more for I was gaining a certain amount of satisfaction recalling what happened all those years ago. It was gratifying to realise how good my memory still is, even though I have reached the grand old age of eighty.

At times while I wrote the memories were so vivid they almost swamped me. On Sunday I had written about the time when I lost my career but I knew that next I must write about an even worse time when my beautiful Fiona was killed. I wondered if I could stand reliving that.

Writing about the first black patch in my life made me feel again the anger and distress I experienced back then and at times I had felt I couldn't continue. I was just thinking this when there was a knock on my door. I have virtually no visitors so knew it must be the delivery boy with my shopping order.

I picked up my scarf from the back of the couch and pulled it over my head and across the lower part of my face before answering the door. I have always considered this need to cover up my aged face absurd, but I must comply with the laws.

I opened the door and standing before me was a smiling brown man, my box of provisions balanced easily on one of his bare arms. He was dressed in the Delivery boy's uniform of khaki trousers and a matching shirt with the sleeves rolled up. His smile revealed a set of beautiful white teeth and I thought what an attractive young person he was. I also thought how absurd the laws are that allow this man to reveal his beauty, while I must conceal my crone's face and withered body for fear of inflaming desire.

He said cheerfully, 'Do you want me to put it on the table for you Missus?'

I answered a muffled, 'No thank you. I can take it.'

Our hands touched briefly as he gave me the box.

I watched as he strolled back to the van whistling, and he lifted his hand in farewell before climbing into the seat and disappearing down my steep driveway.

I carried the box inside and unpacked it before placing it on the verandah for collection next week. I felt strangely disturbed and on edge.

I put away my small supply of food except for an apple and some grapes that I ate for my lunch.

After I had eaten the fruit I made some bread dough and put it in my bread maker. I would have fresh, hot bread for dinner.

I needed to work off the edginess I was feeling so I went outside and threw myself into the physical task of digging over a patch of garden. When this was finished I sprinkled lime over the soil and gently raked it in.

After an early dinner of fresh bread and my remaining piece of cheese I turned on the television. I must do this every night, theoretically to listen to our Master's talk, but I always turn down the sound. I do not wish to hear the ranting of this megalomaniac, and get a twisted pleasure from being able to silence him.

Tuesday

On Monday night I went to sleep easily but woke from a dream, covered in sweat and with my heart racing. It was the first time in many years that I'd had a sexy dream. I would have thought I was long past that sort of thing.

I had been dreaming that Bill and I were on a beautiful, tropical island. There were palm trees, white sand, azure blue water; the typical picture postcard setting. We came in from a swim and then Bill said he would go and get something. I'm not sure why he was going, but as soon as he'd left the young delivery boy came walking along the beach. I was really pleased to see him. He held in his hand a large, round cheese; the kind you used to see in the very best delicatessens.

He sat down on the sand beside me and said, 'I will give you this if you let me make love to you.'

As he said this he ran his hand up my bare arm, and I thought how wonderful it would feel to let him take me on the beach in the sunshine. I put my arms around his young brown neck and then I woke.

I lay in the dark, feeling old and foolish and slightly disappointed. Where had this dream come from? I remembered the slightly edgy feeling I experienced after taking my box of provisions from the boy and recognised I had felt affected by his physicality. While my mind knew he was young enough to be my grandson, my old and faded body had still responded to his beauty and sent subconscious messages of desire to my brain. I felt glad that at least my dreams were private.

As I lay in bed waiting for sleep to come once again I thought that perhaps there might be a point to all this covering of the female form with which we now live. If the sight of bare brown arms in rolled up shirtsleeves could stir an old woman such as I, what must it have been like for young men watching the half-clad girls of past decades?

But then my mind rebelled against those thoughts. I have spent so many years trying to understand the male mind I have become ridiculous. It is not right that women suffer such discomfort because of the perceived weakness of men.

I drifted off to sleep, hoping I would have no more disturbing dreams.

I woke feeling surprisingly refreshed, and showered quickly before putting on a sweater and long, warm skirt. After a quick breakfast of toast and coffee I opened up this file, for I was determined to record the most painful part of my life. Although I found it difficult to write about my sacking, what happened next would be even harder to record. Despite these feelings of trepidation I felt driven to record what happened to our little family. Perhaps I hoped to gain some sort of peace or closure, or perhaps it is just the maundering of an old woman.

Wednesday

Wednesday is the day I always spend at the Women' Centre. I am alone so much of the time I really enjoy these outings. Except for Saturdays, which I spend with Jill and her family, this is the only day that I see other people and catch up with Ruth and Susie.

I'd met these two old friends again when I first started going to the Centre, and learned Ruth had been sacked from her teaching position shortly after Phoebe was killed. She had been accused of being a troublemaker and, like me, offered 'retraining' which she refused. Susie had continued to teach music at the girls' college until she retired.

They had been neighbours for years and were good friends, and we soon became a close trio. For many years now we have met up at the Centre on Wednesdays where we play scrabble and cards and discuss our problems and our families. When there aren't any Carers around we bemoan the way our society has changed, but we are always careful not to be overheard.

I did not tell them about the chance I'd had to escape, for I felt my contact with that part of my family should be kept secret even from these dear friends. I did tell them of how I had sounded off to Jill and my granddaughters, and the consequences. When Amy was taken away I told them about it, and how I feared she had probably been killed. Both of them still had husbands so hadn't realised what happened to widows. They were horrified to hear about Amy and her fate.

Now I was anxious to see if Ruth would be at the Centre today. I was also keen to catch up with Corinne, hopefully on the bus so that I could warn her about the Carers.

When I am at home I usually wear long pantaloons, which are the nearest things to slacks that I can make that are reasonably comfortable for working in the garden. These are not considered suitable attire for outside one's home so I put on a gown. I put a touch of powder on my nose and cheeks and a light lipstick on my wrinkled mouth. I didn't look good, but at least I looked respectable.

It was nearly eight so I grabbed the heavy cloak from its peg in the hallway. I pulled it over my other clothes and adjusted the hood so my hair was covered. I picked up my purse and made sure my identity card was easily accessible for I needed it to get on the bus.

Sometimes the bus is running late but today it was on time. I climbed the steps, tripping on the hem of my cape in my hurry to get on board. I handed the driver my identity card. He pushed it into the slot at the right hand side of his steering wheel, and then asked me my pin number and my code word. When I gave him these he moved aside the metal bar and let me through. The bus was already almost full but I found a seat about halfway up the aisle.

As usual my fellow passengers were mainly women shrouded in their hooded capes, but at the back of the bus there were several Island "boys". Many of them wear the khaki uniform of Delivery boys but a few have on navy overalls, an indication that they work at the Disposal Centre, a stark windowless building on the edge of town.

For a long time I had been curious about what work was carried out there because it is many years since it was used for the disposal of unwanted books and files. Later it was used to get rid of the rubbish that couldn't be recycled but the continual advances in the re-use of material waste had lessened its use for this.

Rumours abounded that it is now used for the secret trials and disposal of people brave or foolhardy enough to challenge our strict laws. After my friend Amy was removed from her home I asked Ali where she would have been taken to.

He told me she would have been taken to the Disposal Centre and that the state would take care of my friend.

His remarks verified what had long been rumoured. Not only troublemakers but also old unwanted women ended their days inside those high, grey walls. The tall chimney that released white smoke into the air during the book-burning years now emits a greyish cloud and a strange smell.

There is a marked difference between the two groups, perhaps a reflection of the work they do. The Delivery boys are always laughing and joking amongst themselves, whereas the others are quieter and appear taciturn and grim. No wonder when you consider the sort of work they must do and the human terror they must witness.

I was thinking about this when the woman next to me said a quiet good morning.

Her voice sounded familiar and when she turned to face me I saw it was Corrine. I asked, 'Are you coming to the Women's Centre again today?'

'Yes,' she answered rather diffidently, 'I enjoyed it so much last week I thought I'd brave this awful bus trip to go again. I get so lonely at times with just my husband for company.'

'I'm glad you have decided to come again. It's at least a chance to get to meet and talk to other women of our age, even if the Carers listen in on our conversations most of the time.'

We settled back in companionable silence while the bus swept down the mountain.

We finally arrived at the Centre after several stops along the way. The "boys" at the back had already been off loaded, the ones in navy overalls at the Disposal Centre and those in khaki at the Delivery Centre.

Corinne and I got off the bus along with several others of our brown-clad companions. We must have looked like a flock of brown hens as we moved in a group towards the sliding doors. As soon as we were inside we removed our capes because this place is off limits to men. Mind you not many men would be interested in coming here, as it is definitely a meeting place for middle aged and older women and the range of entertainments is limited.

A Carer, who I quite like, greeted us at the door. Her name is Sheila and she seems to me to be more genuinely pleasant than the rest of them. All the Carers wear long blue gowns and are big, solid women. Most of them appear to be in their forties but are from different ethnic backgrounds. At times I have wondered how they came to be selected for this job. Was there some common denominator? Did they receive special training to full-fill their mind-numbing duties of spying on a group of elderly women?

There are tables and chairs set up in small groupings around the room. In one area the women knit and sew, in another the card players gather and in the remainder of the room various board games are played. There is also a corner, which we jokingly call the library, where the small collection of books is shelved. Near this are a kitchen and dining area where the Carers serve tea and coffee and sandwiches and cake.

As soon as we entered the hall I looked around to see if Ruth was in our usual spot, but Susie was sitting there alone. I led Corinne across the room to the games area where we three generally spend the mornings playing scrabble. As soon as I was close to her Susie said quietly, 'Gerry died on Sunday.'

I felt a stab of grief. I knew from Ruth that he had been ill for some time, but had not seen him since those long ago days of barbecues and picnics when our children were young. I had continued to picture him as the vital, flirting man he was then and feel saddened to think he is dead, but uppermost in my mind was concern for Ruth. What would happen to her now?

I whispered to Suzie, 'Have the Friends been yet?'

Because she lives next door I presumed she might know how Ruth was.

Susie replied softly, 'I've only seen her to talk to once since Gerry died, and that was on Monday. When I went to her place yesterday a Friend answered the door and said she was resting, so I don't know what's happening. I'm so worried about her. Her son-in-law is in the Civil Service, and he may be able to pull strings so that she can stay in her own home. But somehow I don't think he'll be bothered.'

As we were talking a Carer crossed the room and said, 'Come on girls. Why don't you show our new member how to play scrabble?' She turned towards Corinne and in a jocular manner continued; 'Marion and Suzie are two of our champion scrabble players so you're in tough company.'

I hate the way she always refers to us as girls and the patronising way she talks to us, but I remained silent. We women dislike most of the Carers because we know they are there to spy on us. We pretend friendliness towards them we don't feel. This one, whose name is Midge, is always listening in on people's conversations, and we think she has been responsible for the disappearance of several of the women from the Centre. We are wary about expressing any feelings of dissatisfaction we have about the government and our society when she is near for fear of repercussions.

We smiled false smiles at her, and Suzie, Corinne and I sat down and began setting up the game.

We played several games and then had a light lunch of tea and sandwiches. The Carers know we are friends of Ruth's, and that we would be concerned about her absence. They seemed to be watching us, so we didn't get a chance for a private talk.

During the afternoon we played cards and there was a singer to entertain us. She was a beautiful Island girl with a strong, soulful voice. I felt worried about Ruth and what would happen to her. When Suzie and I were alone briefly in the library corner while we chose our two books for the week I hastily whispered, 'Give Ruth my love if you get a chance to see her, and tell her I'll be thinking about her.'

Corinne and I left the Centre together and caught the bus. As soon as we were seated and the bus was moving she asked, 'Why are you so concerned about Ruth? Won't she go to one of those lovely retreats they have for widows?'

'Not at her age,' I answered abruptly. 'From the little I have been able to find out perhaps some of widows with wealthy sons finish up at those places as well as some of the younger widows. No one talks about what happens to older widows who don't have family members who'll take them in, or ones who don't have influential sons. They are taken away, and no one talks about what happens to them. Within a few days they move a young family into the empty house.'

'But that's dreadful.' Corinne looked at me with a startled look in her dark eyes. 'Do you mean to say that women lose their rights to remain in their own homes once they're on their own, and the older women don't even go to the retreats?'

'That's exactly what I'm saying. Perhaps now you understand why Suzie and I are so worried about Ruth.'

'Well, where do the older widows end up?' Are they put in some sort of old people's homes?'

'For years I didn't know and when a dear friend of mine was widowed I saw her being taken away, as I thought to one of those retreats. I wanted to see if she was all right, and tried to get in touch with her. I asked my son-in-law to help me find out where she was. He told me she would have been taken to the Disposal Centre and that the state would take care of her. I'll never forget the way he sounded when he said that. Since then I'm sure she and others in her position are taken to the Disposal Centre and euthanized. In this society old women are of no use.'

'But why don't people protest about this?

'The ones who are taken have no one to protest on their behalf; and who dares protest in any case?'

Corinne looked horrified and was silent as we swished along the city streets.

As the bus began the steep climb up the mountain she turned to me and said, 'You know Marion, this makes women even more dependent on their husbands than I thought we were. While we were living in the country I worked alongside Ray at lambing and shearing times. I always felt we were a team, and it never bothered me that he controlled our finances. Since we moved to town I have felt more dependent on him, but this is terrible. Because we don't have children, my very life literally depends on him staying alive.'

I sat there feeling guilty. Corinne is only in her mid-fifties and now I had given her this to worry about, perhaps for the next twenty or thirty years. In this case ignorance may have been preferable.

Suddenly she tapped my arm and said cheerfully, 'Well I'll just have to look after that man of mine, and make sure he outlives me.'

Her dark eyes flashed with laughter and I realised why I had felt an instant rapport with her. She is very like my Fiona in looks and mannerisms, and I realised with a shock that if my daughter were still alive she and Corinne would be almost the same age. Oh! How I still miss her so much.

I was thinking this when Corinne broke into my thoughts saying, 'One thing I still don't understand is why it's so necessary to remove these women from their homes and then kill them. Surely they're not that much of a drain on our society.'

'Basically it's because there's still a housing shortage, despite what we are told about the massive building projects that have been undertaken during the past decades. Even though it's nearly thirty years since immigration ceased, the huge population growth in the previous decades put an enormous strain on housing. Now we are getting the Baby Boomers from that time. They're getting married and having families and so, once more, there is pressure on housing availability. In this society it's logical to remove useless old women in order to make way for the young and productive and what is the point of keeping them alive?'

Corinne shuddered beside me, 'My God, I've had no idea about what has been happening. Really Ray and I lived and worked on our land and only worried about the things that affected us. When the price of diesel became prohibitive, when global warming threatened our environment; these were our concerns. Of course we watched the weekly talks on television by our leader and later by his son, but we thought the country was in good hands. I'm ashamed to admit it, but you know neither of us even bothered to vote the last time you could, back in the early thirties. We just lived in our own little world not giving a thought to the bigger picture.'

I patted her shoulder, 'Don't think you've been alone in that. It's what Raman and his cohorts relied on happening, and once his son came to power no one dared question the new laws or protest against anything. I remember Ruth saying years ago, that unless something affects people directly they just don't care, and we're paying now for our self-centredness.'

We were nearing my stop so I said a hasty goodbye and stood up. Unless you're standing and ready to get off the driver is likely to go straight past your stop, and I didn't fancy a long walk down the road.

As I opened the door to my house I heard a rustle, and looking down saw something I had been hoping for during the past week – a letter from Joanna.

I clasped it to my chest the way you would a beloved child or pet. Before opening it I turned on the heater and put on the kettle. I would savour it in comfort.

Once the cup of tea was made I sat down in my armchair and opened the letter. It was long and chatty. She wrote of how hard she was working at the experimental farm where she has been employed since graduating with a degree in horticulture. They are currently attempting to create different environments in which they can grow all kinds of tropical fruits, and are having quite a deal of success. She told me in a previous letter the main aim of their farm was to produce every fruit and vegetable available on the world market, and share what they learnt with the rest of the United European Community.

Thomas had completed his Aeronautical Engineering Degree and is working on his thesis to gain a doctorate. I don't understand the details, but it is to do with increasing the efficiency of solar powered airships.

She wrote that Joe recently retired and he and Monique had bought a smallholding in the Dordogne Region and are very happy. The property already had a small vineyard planted and they plan to extend this.

Although it has been ten years since he remarried, I still feel a little quiver of distaste at the thought of Joe with another woman. I inwardly chide myself for being so ridiculous. He was a young man when Fiona was killed, and it's only natural he would eventually find someone else to love. I'm really glad he did because I loved him too, and I want him to be happy, but I still can't help feeling just the tiniest bit put out that he could replace Fiona with another woman.

Joanna had saved the main news for last. She is getting married to Pierre in December in a tiny church in the village near to where Joe and Monique are now living. I knew she met Pierre at university where they were doing the same course, and that they have since worked at the same farm. Obviously they have a lot in common, and from what Joanna has told me they are very well suited and very much in love.

She ended by saying she wished I could be there to share their big day.

After I had finished the letter I made a sandwich and another cup of tea before settling down to reread it. It was so lovely to hear from her, and to know they are all well and happy.

It was still early evening so I opened up my computer and continued writing my journal. I have completed the hardest part but there are still many events to record.

Thursday

Last night I slept with the letter under my pillow and I dreamt I was at the wedding. I saw Joanna, tall and graceful like her mother, walking down the aisle looking radiantly beautiful. It was a lovely dream and I woke with a sense of wellbeing.

Unfortunately this feeling doesn't last because I think of yesterday, and what has probably happened to Ruth. I am thinking of this when my phone rings. I pull my dressing gown around my shoulders and hurry to the lounge room feeling very anxious. No one rings me except Jill and usually not this early.

I pick up the receiver and say a breathless, 'Hello.'

It is Jill sounding very brisk. 'Hi Mum. Sorry to get you out of bed. Just thought I'd let you know we're headed off to the hospital. Fatima's pains have started.'

'It's a bit early. She's all right isn't she?' I mumble sleepily.

'The baby was due in a couple of weeks, but it seems to have decided to put in an appearance early. Anyhow I'll give you a ring when it's all over.'

I put down the phone and am thinking of Fatima, and hoping that this labour will be shorter than her first, when there is a loud knocking on my door. This is even more disturbing than the early morning phone-call for I rarely have visitors. I feel cross with myself for being caught in my dressing gown. I hurry into my bedroom and replace the dressing gown with my cloak. I run a comb through my wiry hair and push Joanne's letter under the mattress before answering the door.

Standing before me is a tall man dressed in a dark blue suit and a woman wearing a similar outfit to those of the Carers.

He says rather officiously, 'My name is Jones and this is Ms Forsyth.'

He shows me a card and I see the insignia of the Civilians' Services Department on the top before he puts it away.

I feel awkward standing there with my feet bare and my hair a mess, and begin to apologise.

He stops me with a wave of his hand, 'No, no Mrs. Harper we should apologise to you for this early intrusion. I should have contacted you before we came, but we were in the area.'

My mind is in a whirl. Why are these people here? The only times I have been subjected to visits from officials before were when Bill died and after Joe and his little family defected. Can the authorities have somehow found out about my letters from Joanna, or is this something to do with Ruth?

Nervously I show them into the lounge room and excuse myself while I hurriedly put on a long day dress and run a comb through my spiky hair. I don't for one minute believe they just happened to be in this area so early in the morning. I am sure they have come unexpectedly to catch me off guard and make me feel ill at ease. In this they have certainly succeeded, and I hurriedly push my letter further under the mattress and smooth the coverlet.

When I return Mr. Jones is seated with a clipboard on his lap, but Ms Forsyth is wandering around the room.

I think, 'What a stickybeak,' and take an instant dislike to her.

Sounding more relaxed than I feel I ask, 'What is the purpose of this visit?'

Without preamble he says, 'We understand that a short time ago you had your annual physical examination.'

Still mystified I answer, 'Yes, as a matter of fact I did, and the doctor was very pleased with everything so why are you here?'

'Now that you are eighty we need to determine if you are still capable of caring for yourself in your own home.'

I answer sharply, 'It's the first time I've heard of that particular regulation, but I can assure you I'm more than capable of looking after myself.'

Virtually ignoring my comment he continues, 'Do you have someone in to do the housework?'

'Of course not. I'm quite able to look after this little house.'

'Do you mind if Ms Forsyth has a little look around while I ask you a few more questions?'

I want to say I definitely do mind, but that would make me appear uncooperative so I say, 'Not at all.'

I feel very glad I have pushed the letter further out of sight, but am still worried about it. Have they somehow learnt about this secret correspondence? Are they pretending to be checking up on my ability to look after myself as a ruse to search my house for evidence?

'What about meals. Do you have them brought in?'

I hear Ms Forsyth opening cupboards and then the refrigerator, and feel this stickybeak of a woman is violating my privacy. At least she'll see I have plenty of nutritious food on hand. I turn my attention back to Mr. Jones.

'As a matter of fact I quite enjoy cooking, and wouldn't dream of ordering in ready prepared food.'

'What about the grounds. Do you have a gardener or a handyman in to do that for you?'

'No,' I answer, 'I do all the gardening myself, and I grow most of my own vegetables.'

As I am saying this I hear that woman opening the back door. From there she will be able to see my vegetable garden and at present it is flourishing.

He makes marks on his clipboard before continuing, 'Can you remember the name of the high school you attended?'

This is a question out of the blue. I fail to see its relevance to me living alone, but I go along with the charade.

I tell him the name of the high school and then for good measure also name the primary school I had attended as well as the university.

'Do you remember in which years you attended university?'

I tell him this then suddenly he says, 'And what did you do yesterday?'

By now I am getting really annoyed by these stupid questions, but also feeling nervous about where they are leading. Determined not to show my growing fear I answer belligerently, 'I went to the Women's Centre as you probably already know.'

'What did you do there?'

'I played scrabble during the morning and after lunch a few hands of rummy. There was also a short concert in the afternoon with a beautiful Island girl singing some of her traditional songs.'

He fires off another question, 'Whom did you talk to there?'

I am becoming more nervous. What is the hidden agenda behind this visit? I ask abruptly, 'Can you tell me what the purpose is behind these stupid questions ?'

He smiles patronisingly, 'Now don't get upset Mrs. Harper. We have your best interest at heart. I know you passed your physical examination with flying colours, but sometimes, as we get older, we become forgetful. It would appear that your long-term memory is very good, but I need to know if your short-term memory has become impaired. If this has happened it is dangerous for you to live alone.'

Now I can hear the woman moving around in my bedroom. She is opening my wardrobe doors. What is she looking for? Dirty clothes I have taken off and forgotten to wash, or is there some more sinister reason behind this visit? Is she ascertaining how many people could live in my house? I think again of the letter shoved under my mattress and am afraid. I want her out of there.

I say determinedly, 'And what are your qualifications for assessing the state of my memory?'

He mumbles something about simply doing his job but I continue, 'I can assure you I have not become the least bit forgetful, and am willing to undertake a properly administered medical test to prove this. However I am not prepared to put up with any further questioning from someone unqualified to make a professional assessment. Now I would like you and your compatriot to leave.'

They go but before getting into his car Mr. Jones turns to me and says, 'You haven't heard the last of this. We will be back.'

After they leave I sit on the verandah for a while feeling shaken and confused. There had been a definite threat in Mr Jones's last words. I want to ring Jill and tell her of the visit and that I am frightened, but know I won't be able to contact her until after Fatima's baby is born. Giving birth is women's business, and must be carried out in an isolated section of the hospital with no contact to the outside world.

It is only three hours since Fatima went into labour but I ring Jill's number. I get the message bank, so leave a brief message asking Jill to ring me because I am worried about something.

I spend the morning wandering around my garden, pulling the odd weed and deadheading the last of the daisies in my back yard. I have missed breakfast because of my visitors and been too upset to want to eat anything, but by noon I am hungry and make a sandwich and a pot of tea. I sit outside while I have my snack, trying to relax in the warmth of the weak winter sun, but my mind keeps returning to thoughts of my visitors and the threat in Mr. Jones's final, ominous words.

Although Fatima will have only been in labour for about seven hour I ring Jill's number again, hoping that this time she's had a quick birth. Her first was long, but usually second births are much quicker.

With slightly shaking hands I key in her number, wondering if I will once more get the answering machine. After several rings the phone is finally answered, but not by Jill.

A young voice says, 'Hello. How can I help you?'

I recognise the voice of the young Island girl, Shanna, who does some of Jill's housework.

She sounds nervous and is obviously not used to answering the phone so I say gently, 'I'd like to speak to Jill please.'

She answer, 'The mistress is not here. She is with young Missus Fatima helping her have her baby.'

I say less gently, 'I know that but it's been several hours. I thought she might be home by now.'

The young lass says timidly, 'Perhaps Miss Fatima have bad time."

I don't point out that this is pretty obvious, but instead ask her to get Jill to ring me when she returns home, thank her and put down the phone.

I am beginning to feel desperate to talk to Jill, but know this won't be possible until after the baby is born.

Unless I have an emergency I don't like to ring Ali at work, but I feel an urgent need to find out what was behind the unexpected visit by Mr. Jones and his associate.

His assistant answers the phone, but when I identify myself and ask to speak to Ali he says coolly, 'He is in a meeting at present and cannot be disturbed.'

I answer equally coolly, 'Will you please tell him I rang and ask him to ring me back?'

As the hours pass I become more and more frightened when Ali doesn't call. I try twice more to get in touch with him at his office, but each time am told he is not available.

Once it is past five o'clock I decide to wait until he is home and to ring him there. I have felt sick with worry all day, unable to settle to do anything or even to want to eat. By six my head is pounding and my empty stomach rumbling nervously. I make a cup of tea and cook some vegetables and a chicken breast and force myself to eat and drink, hoping this will help me feel strong enough to deal with Ali. I have convinced myself there is some ominous reason for him not contacting me.

At seven I am sure Ali will be home so I ring him there and feel such a flood of relief when he answers. I blurt out crossly, 'Where have you been all day? I've been so anxious to talk to you. I had a visit from a man and woman from the Civilians' Services Department, and they said they'd be back. Do you know why they would come here?'

'Slow down, slow down,' he says impatiently, and I imagine him scowling at the other end of the line.

I draw a deep breath and try to say calmly, 'Ali, I'm frightened. The man asked me a lot of questions about what I could do and what I remembered. I felt I was being threatened, and I haven't been able to talk to Jill about it, and you didn't ring me back. Can you make sure they don't come again?'

For a long time Ali is silent then he says, 'I'm afraid it's rather out of my hands. I've protected you for years, but you have lived such a long time and they have become impatient. The problem is you could live for another ten years, going by your recent medical check up results. The authorities are no longer prepared to allow a lone old woman to take up so much space when a young family could be relocated to your house.'

He sounds so cold and formal. The fear that has been building up in me all day causes my voice to quaver, but I try to sound calm as I ask, 'What will happen to me? Will I have to move in with you and Jill?'

I listen stunned as the man, who has been my son-in-law for so many years, says, 'I think you know the answer to that questions Mother Marion. You living with us would not work out. You are too much of a trouble-maker. For

Jill's sake I have made sure you could stay in your home all these years, but you must accept what is inevitable. It is time for you to make way for the next generation.'

I gasp in horror at what he is telling me. For a long time I have really known that lone women faced euthanasia; now I must acknowledge the prospect of it happening to me and find the thought unbearable.

I cry pitifully, 'Jill won't let this happen to me. I need to talk to her.'

Ali replies abruptly. 'That is impossible. She's still at the hospital with Fatima, helping another new life come into the world. You must accept the inevitable.'

Desperately I cry, 'But I'm not ready to die yet. And what will Jill think has happened to me if I just disappear?'

'She will believe what she is told. Now I must hang up and have my dinner. Goodbye Mother Marion. You've had a long life, and the end will not be painful.'

For a long time after he has rung off I stand there holding the silent phone in my shaking hand, unable to make even the small move necessary to put it on its stand. I remember again Ruth's words about people not really caring about what was happening until it affected them. Her words ring true for I have been as guilty as everyone else in this respect. I had known since Amy was taken away that older women's very lives depended on them having a man to protect them but had accepted this, though sadly, as a part of our society. I feel ashamed.

I have spent the night rereading this journal and completing the record of these last few days. It has been painful remembering the bad times, although there were many joyous memories as well. Now my eyes feel blurry from lack of sleep, and also from the hours I have spent staring at the computer screen. My shoulders ache and my fingers are stiff, but I feel I have recorded a true social history of how Australian women's lives changed during the past century and what life was like for the women of my generation. If my father were still alive I think he would be proud of me.

Epilogue

My name is Marion. I was named after my great, great grandmother on my mother's side of the family.

I had always been quite proud to bear this name because my Nanna Amani said she had been a wonderful woman. I have seen a photograph of her standing in the middle of a prolific vegetable patch. She is dressed in weird-looking pantaloons stuck into long socks and looks a tough old girl.

She died the year my mother Jodi was born. Family lore has it there was something mysterious about her death. Evidently she phoned her daughter, my great grandmother Jill, the day before she died. Great grandmother Jill was assisting her daughter Fatima during a birthing so could not be contacted. She was incommunicado the way one was in those days during the birthing process. Afterwards the girl who had answered the phone told Jill her mother sounded worried.

The next day Marion was found dead, sitting on the verandah dressed in her cloak with the hood lying lopsidedly across her face. This was strange because she hated that cloak and only wore it when she was going out.

On the coffee table inside her house were two packages; one a present for Fatima's new daughter and the other addressed to my Nanna Amani. There was also a crumpled piece of paper in the bin with the words, "Darling Jill, You may not" and a pile of ashes in the sink as though she had burnt some paper. Her computer was on, but everything had been erased.

The authorities said she died of a heart attack, but she had had a physical check up the previous week and her heart had been fine.

I had heard this story, but hadn't thought much about it until the night of the party organised by Mum and Dad and my older brothers to celebrate my graduation in Advanced Technology.

During the evening my Nanna Amani came up to me with a package and said in that quiet, half-apologetic way women of her generation have of speaking, 'I want you to have this. My Nanna Marion left it to me, but I have not known what to do with it. You are such a clever, educated girl you might be able to find out what is on it somehow.'

She handed me the package as if it contained something rare and precious, but when I opened it there was only an old USB stick inside. These were used in the past for data storage but were superseded long ago. I could tell Nanna Amani thought she was giving me a treasure so thanked her profusely, promising to check it out when I had the opportunity.

After the party I put it in a box in the back of my wardrobe and forgot about it. I couldn't imagine there would be anything of importance on it coming as it did from one of the women of the lost generations.

My friends and I have scant respect for the women who came before us. Even our mothers seem to lack our ambition and thirst for knowledge. My mother says they had a poor start to their schooling, but that's just an excuse for their lack of drive. After the Workers' Uprising women were encouraged and given financial assistance to return to study, but few of them took the opportunity

Our mothers are also so much more accepting of the frailties of men than we consider necessary. There is no way we can understand how or why the women of our mothers' generation and those before allowed themselves to be so downtrodden and powerless.

When we were at university we felt so superior to them, for we strode around campus in our boots and trousers to tutorials, where we silenced the boys in the group with our superior knowledge and verbal ability. Later we obtained good jobs, bought our own houses and allowed men to share our lives, but only on our terms.

With the arrogance of youth we laughed at old film clips showing women shuffling along covered from head to foot by those ghastly, heavy cloaks. We sneered at how they hadn't worked to earn a living, instead relying on men to keep them.

In school we had been told of the Workers' Uprising in 2090 and the assassination of Raman the Second. We learnt about John Curtis, the great grandson of an earlier prime minister; of how he desegregated the schools and libraries, removed the dress restrictions women had been required to follow and repealed the laws relating to curfews and meetings. Many members of the National Militia and the Internal Security Force were killed during the Workers' Uprising, and those who survived were sent to the Education Institute to be retrained. People working for the Citizens' Services Bureau were also required to undergo retraining programmes. Under Curtis's leadership our land changed from a restrictive totalitarian society to the free democracy it is today.

Despite knowing about this my friends and I still felt the women of Australia who had gone before us must have been weak docile creatures.

Because I held these opinions I had never even bothered to try to access whatever was on that old USB stick until Nanna Amani became ill. She sent a message through my mother asking me to come to see her.

When I arrived she was very agitated. It was now fifteen years since my graduation party. I thought she would have forgotten about the package she had given me then, but as soon as I entered her room she asked if I had been able to get anything from the old thing. I gathered she thought it might hold some clue to her grandmother's sudden death; a death that had bothered her all these years. She wanted to know what her Nanna Marion had written. Now in her eighty-third year she felt her own death was imminent, and wanted the mystery cleared up before she died.

To calm her down I said I would see what I could do, and later that day retrieved the old USB stick from the box where it had lain all that time.

Because I am now Head of Advanced Technology I have ready access to the Museum of Technology where I was sure I would find compatible equipment.

The museum is situated on campus, so during my lunch break I walked across to it, showed the guard my card and went in search of a suitable machine. It didn't take me long to locate the old computer I needed and I had the guard place it on a desk for me. I booted it up, attached the USB stick to the port at the front of the machine and suddenly these words appeared on the screen. "I know they are coming but don't know how long I must wait; how much longer I shall be allowed to live."

Was this just going to be the maundering of a senile old woman? I scrolled past a few pages and read; "When I raised my eyes again I caught sight of myself in the shop window. I saw a strange, brown bat-like creature scuttling along and realised with a shock that it was my reflection in the glass. I have never got used to the image that I must now display when I am in the outside world."

I held my breath. This was important. I could hear the voice of my great, great grandmother speaking to me from the past, telling me what had happened to her during a time that by this year of 2153 has been lost to history. Those years are not spoken about for it is considered a shameful period in the history of our great land.

I am a speed-reader, but still took quite a while to read the whole document. When I finished I sat for a while thinking over all I had learnt about Marion's life and those of her friends and family. I also thought of her final hours. I imagined her wrapping and addressing the package, beginning to scribble a note to her daughter then changing her mind for fear of causing trouble between Jill and Ali, and finally burning the incriminating letter from Joanna. She must then have erased all she had written on her computer before donning that hated heavy cloak and sitting on the verandah to wait for the return of her executioners. I imagined her watching as her words disappeared from the screen, and thought it must have been a bit like watching her life flash by and disappear into the ether. I don't cry easily, but I felt tears streaming down my face as I re-read that page.

I brushed away my shameful tears, and thought of what I must do with Marion's document. This was a valuable piece of social history and should be available in hard copy.

I called the old guard and said to him, 'Stand here. Don't let anyone touch this computer.'

He clicked his heels and almost saluted, and I wondered if he were an ex- Militia man, one of those men who had walked the streets and beaches and struck fear in my mother's heart when she was a young woman.

I dashed across campus to the resources centre where I booked out a mobile publishing unit. I returned to the museum with it only to discover the connections were incompatible. After examining the old computer I worked out how I could fix this problem and left the museum once more, this time in search of the wiring and jacks I would need.

It didn't take me long to make the necessary alterations; then I turned the computer back on, typed in what I thought a suitable title and pushed the "publish" button. I knew the process would take a few minutes so went for a coffee.

When I returned there was the book in the tray, pristine and complete with the cover title, "Disappearing Women." I picked it up feeling so proud of my namesake. She had lived through such tumultuous, defeating times, but still retained the will and energy to try to set the record straight before she was killed.

I determined her effort would not be in vain, so holding the book tightly to my chest I headed off to show it to my friend, Anna, who is Head of Historical Research.

Biography – Barbara Knight

After many years as a teacher, housewife and mother I completed a Bachelor of Arts at UTAS, majoring in English Literature and History in the 1970s. I followed this with a graduate Diploma in Librarianship and worked in public libraries for sixteen years before my retirement.

During retirement I spent several years attempting to become partially self-sufficient by fishing and growing a huge variety of vegetables and fruits before turning to the more cerebral pursuits of writing and painting.

I am an avid reader, a long term member of book discussion groups and have been writing seriously for many years. I have had six short stories published in anthologies or magazines. I have also written a number of novels and a memoir.

www.ingramcontent.com/pod-product-compliance
Lightning Source LLC
Chambersburg PA
CBHW070553120726
47909CB00007B/2324